THE BAWDY
MRS. GREY

THE BAWDY MRS. GREY

HENRY LEWIS NIXON

CUTTING EDGE

ISBN-13: 978-1-962896-37-5

Published by
Cutting Edge Books
PO Box 8212
Calabasas, CA 91372
www.cuttingedgebooks.com

CHAPTER ONE

WHEN I saw her come out of the building and head for my car I thought she was just another dizzy blonde, but I changed my mind when she got in with me. She wasn't just another blonde. There was something mean about her and she was beautiful. I could tell she had a lot of fire in the furnace when she looked at me and smiled. It was one of those sarcastic smiles that made you want to slap her hard.

But you wanted to kiss her too. You wanted to kiss those big soft lips of hers and then slap her down and kiss her again.

I wished they hadn't assigned this one to me because she was the kind of girl I could make a fool of myself over and I didn't want to be a fool again. I was trying to come clean and stay away from dames awhile, but I didn't tell her to get out. My resistance wasn't that strong. I knew trouble was coming my way, but it would be nice trouble and even if it was a lot of trouble I knew it would be worth it if she was thrown in with the bargain.

"Mike's the name, Mike Callahan."

When I spoke she looked me up and down like she was guessing my weight.

"I'm Kitty," she said and I wanted to make a joke right then, but I figured I'd have to know her for half an hour before I could make jokes like that around her.

"You don't look like the kind of girl who'd be taking driving lessons."

"I used to drive, but I had a bad wreck about five years ago and quit. Now I've decided to try it again."

I explained the double controls to her. There was a steering wheel, an accelerator and everything on her side of the car and there was another set on my side so I could take over if anything went wrong while the student was driving. Chicago's not the easiest place to learn how to drive.

After we got going she took over and seemed to be pretty much at home behind the controls. She relaxed a little and glanced over at me again.

"Come to think of it you don't look like the kind of man who would be teaching driving lessons."

"I'm not the type, but I just got in from L.A. last week and this was the first job I could find. I don't plan to stay in this car jockey business forever if that's what you mean."

I guess she was looking at my heavy build and deep sun tan when she said I didn't look the type. She was right. I wasn't the type, but unfortunately I developed a bad habit in my childhood. I got in the habit of eating and this job was strictly from hunger. A year ago I went to L. A. for a big deal with an army buddy of mine. We were going to run used cars down to Mexico and sell them for a small fortune, but like everything else I had ever tried it didn't work out. We got the deal moving all right, but then some big time crooks got wind of it and moved in. Hal joined up with them, but I pulled out. I never could stand working for a big shot. That's one of the reasons I took this lousy job. I don't have to see much of the boss.

But it was a strictly from hunger job. I took it so I could get the lay of the land in Chicago and move into something big later on.

Kitty was doing fine at the wheel. We went down Montrose to the Outer Drive and then turned north. She stepped down on the accelerator and the Ford we were driving shot ahead like a scared rabbit.

"I've got the hang of it now."

"I hope to God you have," I said and watched the road ahead so I could take over if anything went wrong. When we reached the Foster Avenue cutoff she didn't let up one bit and I thought we'd turn over as the tires screeched around the long curve in the drive.

"My nerves aren't built for this kind of thing."

"You don't look like the nervous type to me."

"Maybe not, but I like to live."

"For what?"

"You got me there, sister, but if you don't mind too much will you slow down a little. There's a stop light ahead."

She stopped the car like she started it, with a suddeness that shook your teeth and then she looked over at me and gave one of her contemptuous smiles that again made me want to hit her.

She drove like a lady as we turned up Sheridan Road.

"Do I pass the test?"

"Either you pass or get another teacher."

"Then I pass."

When we got to the Edgewater Beach Hotel she asked me if I'd like a drink and I said yes before I remembered I only had five bucks to last me the rest of the week. Instead of pulling up in front of the hotel she drove on up the road a couple of blocks and turned into the drive of one of those pre-Roosevelt mansions that lined the Gold Coast.

"You work here?"

"I live here. Good enough for you?"

"If the whiskey's anything like the house it suits me."

She jumped out of the car and ran up the front steps before I could open the door. Sure she was a crazy kid. I figured she was just another one of those spoiled rich bitches who was born with a silver highball glass in her hand, but later I found that I missed my guess. She wasn't born that way. She just got that way and she did it the hard way.

The front door was open when I got there and I wandered in expecting a butler to throw me out at any minute. I stood there holding my beat up hat looking as awkward as I felt. The house was like those you see in the movies, an English castle with a front hall as big as the Palmer House lobby complete with suit of armor standing at attention. I thought all those places had been sold at auction and turned into apartment houses, but there it was for me to touch if I didn't believe my eyes. I started looking at the heavy paintings on the living room wall to have something to do and I was trying to decide why anybody wanted to buy a picture of a table loaded with fruit when she came running down the stairs.

"Like it?"

"It's O.K., but I don't believe my eyes. I thought all these places went on the block during the depression."

"My husband was very lucky."

"Your husband!"

"That's right."

And then for the first time I looked at her finger and saw the wedding band and the engagement ring with a rock as big as Gibraltar. I usually look at the fourth finger left hand on a dame right off, but this girl was so young and so full of hell that I didn't even think of her as a Mrs.

After she told me she was married, she walked up close to me and looked up at me with those bright blue eyes of hers. You can look but you can't touch she was saying. Don't get too close or you'll find out, I was thinking.

As she was mixing the drinks she told me about her and David. He was over fifty when he married her and all the family had objected because they wanted him to be faithful to the memory of his aristocratic family background. Then too, he had diabetes and they had always planned for him to die without a wife to inherit his money. He was the quiet sort who spent all this time mulling over the business details of his chain of hotels.

"In fact that's about all he does do anymore."

"With you around the house I don't see how he keeps his mind on business."

"Remember he's nearly sixty."

"If I was sixty I'd still figure out something."

"I'll bet you would."

We touched glasses and I took a sip and watched her drain the whole glass without taking a breath. The whiskey was so damned expensive that it didn't even taste like whiskey to me. I like for it to burn a little as it goes down, but this whiskey was too cultured for anything like that. I finished mine and asked her to leave the water out of the next one.

"And how did you meet this David?"

"I was a student nurse. One day he went into a diabetic coma and when he woke up the next morning he found me at his bedside taking his pulse. We got to be good friends while he was in the hospital. I was the first person who understood him. He had always been sensitive about his diabetes and because I was nurse he could talk about it with me. Later he asked me out to his house for a swim and when he saw me in a bathing suit there was no longer any doubt in his mind. He needed a wife and he needed me because I understood him."

"For a million dollars I'll bet I could understand him."

"For a million dollars I'll bet you'd do more than understand him."

"Cut the cracks."

We sat down to work on the third drink. Maybe that whiskey had culture and didn't taste like much, but it sure had an Indian kick, the kind that sneaks up on you.

I knew it was getting late and that I ought to be headed back to the office, but the whiskey was free and I didn't want to leave before I got the lay of the land. I began to make conversation with the hope that it would lead up to some kind of invitation. It did because when I asked her what she did all the time she told me that she led a very dull life. David was jealous of her and thought that the best way to keep her safe was to give her only five dollars a week allowance.

"So I spend most of my time painting figurines."

"Figurines?"

"Sure you know, china dolls."

"This I got to see to believe."

"Don't I look the type?"

She batted her lashes at me again.

"Somehow I can't picture it."

"Then I'll prove it to you."

She took my hand and led me back out into the hall and up the winding staircase to the second floor. She had one of these things I guess you would call a studio. Anyway it was a room cluttered up with a lot of china dolls sitting on a work bench. There was an easel in the room and some half finished clay statues and out of the corner of my eye I saw a comfortable day bed over by the window.

She held one of the white clay figurines up for me to see.

"I buy them at the dime store. You see a girl can't do much on five dollars a week."

I didn't give a damn about those china dolls, but I pretended to be interested as hell in them. I could feel something stirring up in me and my hand trembled a little as I held the doll. It was the same forbidden feeling I had when I was debating whether or not to kiss my first girl.

"You like them?"

She was standing close and she knew she was making it tough for me. I wondered what she felt. What would happen at the Lake Shore Driving School if they got a complaint about me? I didn't care. There were other jobs and you didn't run into a girl like this every day.

"They're O.K."

I was so choked up I could hardly talk and I knew that I would die if I didn't make a pass at her. It had to be *yes* or *no*. I couldn't stand the waiting any longer.

When I put my arms around her and tried to kiss her she turned her head away and I had to use all my strength to pull it back around so I could kiss her. Then I knew why she was protecting her lips so, because when I kissed her it was like pulling the gate open at the Grand Coolie Dam. She was all over me. It was like she knew all along if I ever kissed her school would be out.

I ran my hand up and down her nice soft arm and she shivered like her old man had turned her out in a snow storm.

"Baby, you like it?"

"Oh, God, how I like it. You're so tough and manly. It's like being held by a giant. I couldn't stop you if I wanted to."

She was mine. I knew it the minute I pushed against her big juicy lips. Now I was going to play with her awhile and make her beg a little. I could afford to take my time, tease her a little now that I had her score. I took little bites of her lips, first with my lips and then with my teeth. I pushed harder until I could feel a deep moan come out of her.

"You like it?" I whispered.

"Oh, Mike, I love it. I just love it. Please. Now."

"How long have you loved it?"

"Since I was a little girl."

"You've always wanted a man?"

"Yes, yes, since I was twelve years old I've wanted a man just like you."

Her lips were pushing against mine. After I kissed her again her hips started making little circles of pressure and then bigger circles of pressure.

"Mike, please don't make me suffer any longer. Oh, I want to, I want to, I want to, please have mercy on me …."

I carried her over to the day bed and let her fall there. Her skirt was up above her knees showing me the prettiest sights I'd ever seen. I'd been places and had things, but nothing like this. Class, real class like this rich bitch and passion didn't usually go together. Now I had it all right there on the couch waiting for me.

She was taking off her shoes, but she was too slow for me. I reached up under her skirt, caught her girdle and pulled, dragging the girdle, stockings and shoes all off with one sweep of my hands.

"Mike darling, don't hurt me."

"I'm not going to hurt you too much, you little bitch," I said. "I'm going to hurt you just enough to be interesting. Don't you like a little pain? Don't all women like a little pain?"

"Oh, Mike."

Kitty made love like she drove the car, wild and fast. She wanted to so bad that I felt like we were both doing each other a favor.

"I'll see you in class tomorrow, teacher."

"Yeah, and we'll have lesson number two."

"Am I a good pupil?"

I said she was but if I had told the truth I would have said she didn't have anything to learn.

When I left the house I felt like a guy who had spent a week in a turkish bath.

That night I didn't do any drinking or carousing around. After supper I went to my crummy room over on Kenmore and got in bed. I hadn't slept that well since I was a little boy.

I'd give you ten to one my Kitty slept well, too.

CHAPTER TWO

MAYBE she felt guilty or something, I don't know what it was, but she didn't show up for a driving lesson the next day. In place of her I had a nervous old maid school teacher. She spent the afternoon trying to kill us both in the car and all the time I was watching the traffic I was thinking about Kitty.

Things like Kitty just don't happen to a guy every ten years but by the time the week passed I had put her back in the part of my brain I reserve for happy memories.

Then big as life she showed up again. After waiting a few days maybe women get a head full of memories just like men.

"I thought you'd given up driving."

"It was dangerous."

"But now you think the danger's worth it?"

"You're worth a lot."

She squeezed my hand and looked at me with those big blue eyes. I knew she had been remembering, too.

Instead of tearing up the Outer Drive like she did before, she drove on down Montrose to the beach.

For a while we just sat there watching the people go by with arms full of blankets and supper baskets as they headed down to the beach. It was the last of May and we were having the first hot weather of the year. Lake Michigan looked cool and green and I felt like we were a couple of kids playing hookey from school to go fishing.

We got out of the car and walked down to the edge of the water. She looked up at me again and took my hand as we went on down past the crowd to the point of sand that jutted out into the water. It felt good being close to her again. There was something right about us. We were both young and full of life and we belonged together like that, walking along the beach on a hot May afternoon. When I thought about her being cooped up all the time with that sick old husband of hers it nearly made me sick.

And it was the same way with me. I was young too and full of life and it wasn't right that I should be at loose ends and not have a woman of my own. If you didn't have a woman when you're young when in hell was the time to have one? And it was the same way about money. Sometimes I watched the rich old dames with the chauffeurs driving them around downtown and thought to myself that it wasn't right. What could dried up old gals like those care for money? Money was made for young people who still knew how to enjoy it.

Hell, the old people had everything and we who were young had nothing. That is we had nothing but sex and before Kitty and I met we didn't even have that, at least not regularly.

We walked on back to the shore and lay down on the grass near a tree.

"Are you happy?" I asked.

She lay on her back and looked up at the white clouds passing over the deep blue sky. It was like she didn't recognize the word.

"You made me happy. I wasn't happy till I met you. I was cooped up in a prison and I could feel everything inside me drying up."

"But you've got lots of money."

"Five dollars a week."

"But look at the place you live, servants, good food, class."

"They don't mean anything."

"Then why did you marry him?"

"I thought they meant something. I thought living in a house like that was all any girl could ever want. And I felt sorry for David."

Suddenly I felt sorry for Kitty. She had everything and she had nothing. She wasn't mean like I had thought at first. She was just a lost kid.

I felt even more sorry for her that afternoon when I took her home.

Her husband was pudgy and bald headed and limped around the living room like a dog sick with the mange. I mean you wanted to shoot him to get him out of his misery. You could tell by his face that he wasn't any happier than Kitty and me. He kept mumbling about his sore foot and then he called in the butler and dressed him down because the chauffeur had quit.

"I don't know when people will learn that they have to work for a living," he was saying to the butler when we went in. "I gave Frank a good room and a good salary and now he leaves without giving any notice."

"That's the way those chauffeurs are," Karl was saying.

"David, this is Mr. Callahan. He's giving me driving lessons."

I shook his fat soft hand.

He kissed Kitty on the cheek and I winced to see his fat red lips that close to her. My mind made pictures of the fat man with his beautiful young wife and I knew I had to get away from there.

Yes, I felt sorry for Kitty all right.

We all sat down and Karl served the before-dinner martinis.

"Mr. Callahan is a wonderful driver. Maybe you could talk him into being our chauffeur. He could go on giving me lessons."

When she said that I could almost see the smile she had inside her.

"Would you consider the job, Mr. Callahan?"

"I don't like my present job."

"I'd see to it that you were well paid and there's a very comfortable room over the garage that goes with the job. You could take your meals here in the house. Uniforms would be furnished and every cent you made would be pure profit."

"It sounds good."

I didn't like the idea of dressing up in a monkey suit, but then I would be near Kitty and then too I thought he would have a Caddy and a Caddy is the only thing in my book that can come near a beautiful woman.

"What kind of car do you have?"

"Most of your work will be driving the Cadillac. Of course we have a station wagon and another light car, but you won't have much to do with them." He paused a minute like he was trying to think of all my duties. "We have a yacht too. Sometimes you'll be needed to help out there. You aren't afraid of water?"

"No, sir," I said. I hated to say *sir* to him in front of Kitty, but then you sort of automatically say *sir* to a man who has three cars and a yacht.

"You look like a good man. I'd like to see you take the job."

I thanked him and told him I would let him know in a few days.

Kitty walked to the front door with me.

"Please take it for my sake, Mike."

"You mean that?"

"Of course I mean it. We can be together every day."

She took my hand in hers and squeezed it and I suddenly felt sorry for her again. Then she stood on her toes and gave my cheek a quick kiss.

"Please."

"It will be dangerous as hell."

"But wonderful."

"God knows how it'll end."

"I love you."

"How can you know?"

"I can feel it down here."

Instead of touching her heart she touched her stomach, but then maybe that's the kind of love we had for each other and maybe that's the only kind of love that's really love.

"I'll give you a ring tomorrow."

"And remember that I love you and that I want to be near you always."

"How can I forget?"

I kissed her and ran down the steps two at a time and got in the car and shot it out into the traffic on Sheridan Road.

That night as I ate my usual fifty-five cent supper at the Marquis Lunchroom on Lawrence Avenue she was still with me begging me to take the job so I could be with her.

But the thing inside me that told me it was dangerous as hell was still with me and it turned my stomach into a leather bag and it made me a little dizzy just to think of the two of us spending the afternoon together in my clean room over the garage. We had tasted love together, but it was only a quick taste. We still had the world of love ahead to explore together.

And the thought of love was all the better because it had the sweetness of the forbidden fruit and forbidden fruit is always the sweetest. It was like being a kid again. Was there ever anything more exciting than forbidden moments? And if you took the excitement away from life what did you have left?

I couldn't finish the food.

I didn't want to think about Kitty anymore that night. I wanted to get slightly drunk.

It was just another ironical trick of life that I drove around in a car all day and then had to take an El when I wanted to go someplace at night.

I went to Danny's joint on North Clark Street. He's another one of my buddies I met while I was making the Sahara Desert safe for democracy. Only he was smart when he came home. He got one of these G.I. business loans and opened a crummy little bar on Clark Street. He made money selling rot gut to bums at twenty cents a throw and when he had half as much capital saved as any sensible business man would need, he opened a strip joint next door.

It seems like the guys like Danny that don't have any sense are the ones who make all the dough in this country. He's like these Texas millionaires you're always reading about. They get a third hand set of drilling tools and go out to some God forsaken desert and start drilling holes in the ground like a gopher that's gone crazy. They get one little well and then they start drilling more holes and the first thing you know these dumb jerks that never had anything in their lives are riding around in Caddies filled with champagne and Texas broads.

Well, that's the kind of guy Danny is. He's got so little sense that he don't know you can't open up a new business on a shoe string.

I pushed open the door at his place and walked in big as day and took a seat at the horseshoe shaped bar that was crowded with conventioneers and just everyday degenerates.

"Take it off, take it off," they were calling to the little blonde who was dancing not two feet from their noses. They were beating on the bar with their beer bottles and acting like they don't know she's going to peel. When I didn't get excited and beat on the bar with my beer bottle, the little queer sitting next to me started giving me the eye so I beat on the bar like all the rest of the degenerates. Who said it was a free country?

By the time the little girl had herself loose for some exercise I saw Danny come out of the back room. He walked past me and I stopped him.

"How's the harem manager?"

"I'm eating and that's more than I can say for some suckers."

"But I don't all the time have to worry about catching something."

We were good friends, but I hadn't seen him since coming back from L. A. He asks me to come in the office for a drink.

You should have seen his office. It was so ritzy that the president of the Bank of America would feel like a country hick there.

"Danny, you've got quite a front here."

"That's how you make the money me boy."

"You talk like that's all there is in the world."

"That ain't all but that's the second most important thing."

He leaned back in the chair to give his beer pot a rest and lighted the stinking Havana cigar he was smoking.

"How come you ain't still in L. A.?"

"That damned house of queers!"

"I heard you liked the coast."

"I did but Hal and I got flim-flamed by some New York sharpies. They found out we had a good racket running cars into Tia Juana and those boys don't let any good rackets stay in private hands. We turned them down at first, but their strong arm boys made it clear as rain water that we'd get snubbed out if we didn't play ball. Hal joined up with them but I got out. I don't want any trouble like that. A little private racket's one thing, but playing with the big boys is something else again. If you get tired playing in their league they won't let you quit. I don't want any job I can't quit."

"What you doing here?"

"I'm teaching dames how to drive at the Lake Shore Driving School."

He didn't say it but I could tell from the look in his eyes that he was thinking I was just another guy that would never amount to anything and maybe he was right.

"I might work you into something down here."

"Legitimate work?"

"Almost."

"I'm going straight. I've seen too many of my buddies start out with shady deals and end up in the big house."

"And I've seen too many suckers like you up in the poor house."

"At least they got dames there."

"Yeah, they got dames but not the kind I got."

While we were talking the door opened and in walked one of his blonde strippers. Her face was still young and pretty and there weren't any marks on it yet from the kind of life she led. Funny how it takes them a year or two before you can see it in their faces. This girl wasn't more than seventeen and I'd guess she was straight in off of some Iowa farm. When young girls like that start going to hell, they go in a big way. And Danny was just the man to help them.

"We going out to eat?" she asked.

Her voice was still soft.

"Meet Mike Calahan. Mike this is Pepper."

"Glad to know you."

"We going out to eat like you said?"

"Sure thing, baby. Where do you want to eat tonight?"

"Cugart's playing at the Marine Room."

I finished the drink and asked him if he would give me a lift as far as the Edgewater Beach Hotel where they were going for dinner.

You should have seen the car Danny had waiting out front for him. It was one of these cream colored Caddies with a convertible top. Jeez, when she pulled away from the curb you felt like you were riding on a cloud.

They let me out at the corner. I think Pepper had asked him to when she whispered something in his ear as we were leaving. She didn't want the doorman to see her ride up with me in the car.

I stood there on the curb and watched Danny pull away in his Caddy with the little blonde's arm around his neck and it got me way down deep. I didn't envy Danny, (that's a lie, of course I did) but at least what I got I got without putting those little country girls up on the block for a bunch of degenerates to leer at. But Christ, I didn't have anything. Not a damn thing.

Maybe I did have one thing. Maybe I had Kitty. She was so beautiful and young and clean that she was like something in a dream. She was so much better than me and the kind of people I knew. She was like a drink of spring water after months of drinking water purified with G.I. chlorine tablets. Kitty was the real thing and I was lucky to find someone like her. At first I had thought she was mean. But I was wrong. She was too young to be mean.

When I walked up the four flights of steps to my bare room I opened my trunk and took out a fifth I kept stashed away there where the landlady couldn't find it. I sat down on my thin mattressed bed and unscrewed the top of the liquor bottle. Out of habit I wiped the top off with the palm of my hand and then turned the bottle up and gurgled down about five good shots. Then I put the bottle down on the floor beside me and lay down on my squeaky bed to think. I couldn't think. All I could do was see pretty pictures of Kitty floating past me. She was so pure and healthy and right. I'd cut off my right arm up to here for her.

As the man said I'd have slaved for her all day just to smell her perfume.

I tried to talk myself out of taking that job as a chauffeur because I was afraid it would mean trouble, but I didn't have a very strong argument with myself. The pretty pictures of Kitty kept interfering with my arguments. Like I said before I never did get along working for big shots, but I couldn't let that stand between Kitty and me.

But if I had been smart I would have dropped the whole thing like a chunk of brimstone.

CHAPTER THREE

"THIS PLACE gives me the creeps," Kitty said.

"It's not a bad room. The springs don't squeak; there's a rug on the floor. It's a lot better than the one I had on Kenmore."

"But it's too close to everything."

Kitty was on my bed beside me. She reached over to the night table and pulled out a cigarette.

"We can't have everything."

"Can't we?"

"What do you mean?"

"Nothing. I was just thinking."

"Nobody ever has everything. We got the most important thing. We're together."

"We can never be together as long as David is alive."

I knew what she meant. His picture kept coming up in my dreams. He was always walking up the steps to my room over the garage, opening the door and finding Kitty and me in bed together with our bodies clinched. But I didn't like the way she used the word "alive." There're some things you think about but don't ever say out loud.

We had made love and were lying beside each other on the bed, our hips touching so the magnetism or whatever it was we felt could flow back and forth between us. I shifted a little and put my head on a pillow so I could look down at her body. She had on just the right amount of make up, enough to make her pretty, but not enough to see. All the lipstick had come off her big lips and there was a drop of blood resting there from where I had bit her a little too hard.

There was that gentle swelling of her arms that tappered down to long fingers with blood red nails. You could tell she never dipped them in anything stronger than cream.

Her breasts were so young and firm they stood up tight even while she lay there on her back and the tips were neat and pale pink, the sure way to telling a real blonde.

When your eyes went down a little further you could see how her stomach sucked in and fell away from her rib cage and even her dimple was deep and perfect. Her legs and thighs might be a little too large for some men, but they were the kind I dreamed about. There was enough in her hips so you didn't have to worry when she got ready to push her babies out. The legs went down to small ankles which reminded me of the tense kind of strength you see on a race horse with the tendons standing out like they were pulled up by a spring.

She was studying the ceiling above the bed but I could tell from the way she was wiggling her foot that she had something else on her mind. After a while she turned her head and looked at me.

"Mike, we've got to stop."

"What do you mean?"

"We can't go on seeing each other like this."

"Don't start getting soft on me."

"I can't help it. I can't spend my days here with you and then go to him at night and have him put his fat arms around me."

She was hitting below the belt when she painted that picture for me. I had almost thought of them together like that too, but every time my mind came close to thinking about it, I shifted over to something else. It made my stomach rumble to hear her talk about it.

"And you want to break it off between us just like that?"

"I don't want to. I love you, Mike and I don't want to ever break it off with you, but not many women can love two men and keep clean."

"You told me you didn't love him."

"I don't, but you know how it is. After all I am married to him. He does things to me. Dirty things I don't want to talk about."

When she said that I was suddenly as hot as a T model Ford climbing Pike's Peak.

"What do you mean?"

"Mike, you aren't a child."

"Then let's leave. Get your things together and we'll pull out. I can get a job in L. A."

"What if it would wear out?"

"I don't get you."

"What if we don't really love each other? Maybe it's just an infatuation with us and if it were to cool off you'd leave me and then where would I be?"

"I love you."

She didn't say any more. She just took long drags on her cigarette and looked far away into space.

When it was four o'clock and time for me to go downtown and pick up David we got dressed. She kissed me and opened the door.

"This is the last time, Mike. I love you but I can't go on like this."

"Wait a minute. Let's talk this over a little more before you say that."

But she ran down the steps and cut around the edge of the garage without looking back at me.

This was not going to be an easy one to charge off the books. Some girls you could have for a night or a year and just wipe them off your mind like wiping chalk off a blackboard, but Kitty wasn't that kind of a girl. Looking back on it now after all these months it's hard for me to say what she had that was different from other girls. I guess maybe it was her spirit that made her different, that and the way she would look at me—like I was the only real man in the whole world. Yeah, Kitty was different from other girls and it wouldn't be easy to charge her off the books.

I drove the Cadillac down to the Palmolive Building on Michigan Avenue to pick up David. (I had talked about him to Kitty so many times that even now I think of him as David instead of Mr. Grey.) When I saw him come limping out of the building I jumped out and held the door open for him.

"Mike I want you to take me by the doctor's office before we go home."

"Yes, sir. I hope you aren't feeling worse today."

He must have felt worse because he began talking about his ailments and it was the first time he had ever mentioned them to me.

"I'm afraid I don't feel very well."

He paused for a minute and then went on.

"From your place you must look upon me as a very lucky man, but believe you me we all have our problems. I guess I'm rich and I live in a twenty room house and I have a charming wife, but I have diabetes."

"I'm sorry to hear that, sir."

"Yes, I have my troubles too. I have an ulcer on my right leg. That's what makes me limp. Diabetics have a tendency to ulcers on the extremities and when they come it's next to impossible to cure them. They might have to amputate my leg."

"I'm sorry, sir. I hope the doctor will have good news for you today."

"Thank you, Mike."

As I drove on through the five o'clock traffic on the Outer Drive I was thinking about this poor bastard in the back seat. I couldn't help but wonder how long he would live and I remembered what I had thought when I first saw him. He was a poor miserable man and like a mangy dog, he would be better off dead. Then I thought about the stinking ulcer on his leg and I thought about him making Kitty sleep in the same bed with him in spite of his rotten leg, but you can't think thoughts like that and stay sane so I put it out of my mind.

After he came out of the doctor's office he seemed to be in better spirits.

"The doctor wants me to take a trip."

"That sounds good, sir."

"It's just the thing for me. I need to get away from it all for a few weeks."

"Where are we going, sir?"

"Hot Springs. He thinks the change would be good for my leg and you know he might be absolutely right."

"I'd like to get away for a while myself."

"That's good because I'll want you to drive me down."

I could see pictures of Kitty and me together again. Down there I would have a regular room in the hotel and she wouldn't worry so much about being caught. He would be taking the baths and stuff and it would give both of us a lot of free time. I thought that I could get Kitty to depend on my loving so much that she couldn't do without it if I just had her with me for a few more weeks. We could run away together, just drop off the face of the earth and it would be wonderful. Dames are all the time hesitating about running away or sleeping with a man or doing anything like that but if you work on them long enough most of them will come around to your way of thinking.

When Karl rang my room that night about nine o'clock and told me that Mr. Grey wanted to talk with me, I thought he was going to tell me all about his plans for the trip.

He was seated in the overstaffed chair by the fireplace reading the Wall Street Journal when I came in. Kitty was on the sofa with her legs drawn up under her, reading a magazine. She didn't look up at me. It was like she was afraid to look me straight in the eye. For a crazy moment I was afraid she had told David about our affair. Kitty was a flighty sort of girl, the kind you couldn't always depend on and that's just the type who would run home and tell daddy about the nasty old man.

"We've decided to leave tomorrow for Hot Springs."

"That's fine, sir."

"But Mrs. Grey has talked me out of driving down. She thinks it would be better for me to fly. I telephoned my doctor and he agreed with her, so we won't need you for the trip. I'll rent a car down there if I want to go out anyplace."

It seemed funny that he should explain to me why he didn't want me to drive him. I guess it was because one chauffeur had quit on him and he didn't want to take any chances on losing me.

"You can stay around the house and take it easy until we come back in about two weeks."

"Thank you, sir. Will that be all?"

"That's all, Mike. I might add that I've been very pleased with your services and that it's not because of you that I'm flying down."

Yes it is, but you just don't know it, I thought.

I tried to catch Kitty's eye before I left the room, but she didn't look up from the magazine in her lap.

It looked like our affair was really ended. Maybe she was one girl who meant it when she said *no*, but if she was it would be the first girl I'd met who was that way.

Anyway, her going away did something to me. It was like I had owned the whole world for a month and then suddenly had it jerked away from me and given to somebody else. I don't know why I was fool enough to let it hurt me so much. I was thirty years old at the time and I had knocked about the world a good deal. I had known women by the hand full and I tried to make myself believe that Kitty was just another skirt in my life.

But like I said before she did something to me that no other woman ever did. Kitty was sc clean and above me that having her made me feel like I really had something for the first time in my life. I was lonesome as hell after she left.

And then something else happened to make things worse. That bastard of a valet named Karl starting riding my butt and after a few days I knew why the other chauffeur had quit.

Karl was the butler and the valet and was the one who really ran the house. He was a tall man with a dark soul. There were deep circles under his eyes and you could never guess what he was thinking. His hair was cropped short and he still had a trace of his German accent.

Karl took over after David and Kitty left. The next morning when he called me and asked me to come to the house for a talk you would have thought it was his house. He was sitting in the boss' chair by the fireplace smoking a cigar. I thought he had called me in so he could send me to the store to pick up something for lunch, but he had something else in mind.

"I saw Mrs. Grey coming down from your room the other day."

"Maybe she was looking for me."

"I saw you come down a few minutes later."

"And what does that prove?"

"Mr. Grey is a very jealous man."

"I don't blame him."

"Let's not play games."

"All right, what are you getting at?"

"If you want to keep your job I'd suggest you leave Mrs. Grey alone."

"I don't know what you're talking about."

"I hope not."

You could tell he didn't believe me. But I was pretty sure he didn't have anything definite on us or he would have gone to Mr. Grey. That was the last thing I wanted him to do. After all, I was sure David would fire me if he had even the least suspicion and I wanted to keep the job. If I had a few more weeks with her I was certain I could talk her into running away with me. If it hadn't been for her I would have told him to take the job and do you-know-what with it.

No, he wasn't sure about anything, but he was sure enough to make life hell for me and know that I wouldn't go to David and complain about it. I guess all of us have a sadistic streak in us and if we got the chance we'd probably all enjoy giving some poor guy hell. Well, Karl had me and he knew it. He made my life hell. First he told me that there was some heavy work to do in the house and had me down on my knees waxing and polishing the hall steps by hand. I took my time about it, but I didn't complain any. I thought it was just a trick to show me who was boss. When I finished that I went up to my room for a nap and the first thing I knew he was on the phone telling me that there was more work to be done.

"You think this is going to be a vacation just because the boss is on a trip?"

"He told me about my duties when I came to work for him and he didn't say anything about polishing the hall stairs."

"But he told you that I run this house?"

"No."

"Then I'm telling you now. I want you to wash the basement windows and then scrub the floors."

The basement was about as big as the Chicago Stadium and it was plenty dirty, but I went to work on it. It was June then and the basement had a musty odor about it that almost smothered me. I was sure I'd catch something down there, but nothing happened. All week I kept at it till I could feel the dirt in my lungs. By the time Saturday night came around I was mad and tired and when I get mad it makes me want a woman. I just couldn't stand waiting till Kitty came home. Maybe I could have waited if I had been sure she was coming back to me. It was either go out on the town or blow my top and take a punch at Karl.

CHAPTER FOUR

'M LIKE other humans, but in a way I'm different, in an important way. When the rest of humanity dreams about doing things and thinks about things that's the end of it. They don't actually ever do those because something inside them holds them in place. That something is missing in me. I dream about making love to a girl and I think about it till it gets so strong that it's just like real and then nothing holds me back and I do it.

It had been that way with me all week. Karl had almost worked me to death and Kitty had left me. I was mad and as the week went past the hate grew inside me like a black flower that opens up in the night. And the more hate I felt the worse I had to get drunk and have a woman. It was the only thing I knew that would make me feel clean again. Some people can get clean by praying or confessing or knocking a golf ball, but I'm not that way. Maybe I could have gotten clean that way too if I had learned it from the start, but I never learned how to confess or play golf and I get rid of my bad feeling the best way I can.

Maybe I picked it up from my mother. She ran a gin mill over on the west side and my first memories go back to her tavern and all the people sitting at the bar on Saturday night and laughing and playing the juke box. And when the laughs were all out they'd start playing with me. They'd start off by giving me beer and then they'd damn near rupture themselves laughing when I'd get enough beer in me to stagger around the room. That's how I got this burn on my left shoulder. One night they got me dizzy and I staggered into the wood stove that heated the joint. But maybe that was funny too, I don't remember.

I did a stretch for six months back in 1940 before I went in the army. It was one of these fancy jails in California where they have baseball teams and all that kind of stuff. This jail was so fancy they even had a psychiatrist to talk to all the prisoners once a month.

After I'd been in this jail about a week they took me up to his office and told me to sit down and wait for the doctor. I was surprised when he treated me like a human and it seemed like he was sort of a queer or something because he just sat there and talked to me. He asked me all kinds of silly questions like where I came from and how far I went to school.

"I don't know who my old man was," I said and I thought he'd kick me out then, but he didn't do a thing but just sit there and wait for me to go on talking. Anyway, this grey-haired doctor and I got to be pretty good friends before my stretch was over and on the day before I left he called me up to his office to tell me good-bye. I asked him why he was interested in me and he said I was an interesting case.

"What do you mean case?" I asked him.

"You are a person who hasn't really grown up."

"I don't get you, doc."

"You see when we are growing up our ego develops so that we are able to distinguish between fact and fiction. We learn to control the primitive part of our personality and not act out on our phantasies. You are what we call a psychopath."

Now I'm sure that psychiatrist knew a lot about me. I couldn't figure out all he said and I don't guess there are many people who could, but I'm sure it was important.

When Saturday came I called Danny and asked him to fix me up with a date. You might not think Danny and I were good friends but we were in a special way. He somehow represented all that was bad in me and when I was in a bad mood like I was that day, he was a very good friend of mine. Later when I would get it all out of my system I wouldn't like him at all, but then I knew that the whole cycle would repeat and I would want him as a good friend again. The difference between Danny and me was that Danny was all bad. He made a profession of his badness and mine was just a hobby.

"You want something extra nice?" he asked me.

"I could do it justice tonight."

"I got a new girl down here who's got a sister. How would you like that?"

"It suits my mood right down the line."

"I'll give them a ring. You meet me here at the strip joint about nine."

Karl paid me that afternoon and I went down to the Loop and bought a grey summer suit that had real class. After supper I went to one of these double features at the Roosevelt where everybody gets shot up and where the good guys win over the bad guys at the end.

When I got to Danny's joint the place was just opening up. A flat chested girl who was the M. C. was standing up there on the stage making cracks about her flat chest and stuffing a handkerchief down in the top of her dress and strutting around like she suddenly had something in her dress.

Danny was in a good mood and got up from his desk to slap me on the back when I came in. It always made him happy to find someone who felt the same way he did about the girls. Maybe it made his conscience lighter and made him feel like a better man when he found somebody else who's as low as he is.

"Fran's on next. We'll go out front and watch her do her stuff."

"Is Fran the girl you were talking about?"

"That's the baby. She started working here last Tuesday. Best girl I've had here this year."

We went out front by the bar where Danny ordered a drink for both of us and insisted that I join him in the doubtful pleasure of smoking a stoggie.

"That M. C.'s a slut if I ever saw one."

"She's queer as a Chinaman eating spaghetti, but she keeps the customers entertained."

After about five minutes the M. C. ran out of jokes about her flat chest and motioned for the boys in the band to announce the next number.

"I'm sure you boys heard about Fran Sims," the M. C. said in her harsh voice. "If you think I got it wait till you see her."

The music blared again and Fran walked out on the stage. She wasn't as young as some of the others, you could tell from the way she walked that she'd been around, but you could also tell she was the kind of girl who would hold up under it. She had long legs like in the Petty drawings and they were the hard legs of a dancer. You could see the long muscles stand out as she walked around in her high heel shoes. And she walked with a cocky air like a marionette pulled in quick movements by a string up above. At first she just walked around the edge of the stage that projected out into the room. She looked down at the faces below her like she hated them all and was going to torture each one individually. She was going to undress the most seductive way she knew how and she was going to dance around out there for the boys and then she was going to quietly walk to the edge of the stage and leave them with nothing but the taste of cotton in their mouths. That was her revenge on man.

Fran did a whirling dance as the orchestra played slow music and then casually she began taking off her gloves and it was funny seeing what that could do to an audience. I guess it was the first thing that started the old chain reaction going and that's why it got them when she casually peeled off her gloves, danced to the back of the stage and gave them to a nigger girl waiting there for them.

The music picked up its tempo and she danced faster. The damned degenerates sitting around the bar started calling out "Take it off, take it off," and beating on the bar with their beer bottles. Now she smiled a little, a mean smile that said "Now you guys have started to suffer. I'm going to put you through hell and then leave you to go back to your empty rooms where you won't be able to sleep from thinking about me. I'll make you suffer the lonely hell that scum deserves."

But as they watched her take off her evening dress and then turn away from them and take off her bra and then turn back to them with her breasts swinging in cadence with the fast music, as they watched her bare from the waist up dancing before them, they did not suffer. They grinned up at her and thought, "Now you cheap little bitch take it off up there and throw it around in front of us and show the whole world that you're nothing but a bitch."

And that was the way the woman made the men suffer and that was how the men made the woman suffer and neither one was really suffering. The woman and the men were both doing it to get rid of that same feeling that I had. Some take it out in exercise and some take it out in drinking and some take it out in watching.

Now the music was hard and the deep-throated drum beat out a rhythm that was discovered in the jungles a million years ago and Fran danced faster. Then she started pumping it up and down. The tempo of the drums increased and the whole room shook from the sex and the drums and the pumping hips and then the naked girl pumped again and held it for a long time and then fell down on the floor in a convulsion as the drums reached their climax and a trumpet suddenly blared out from nowhere and all the lights went off so that the girl and the men were alone with their naked thoughts of full hips and hot naked flesh and jungles a million years old and drums that beat in your stomach.

And I took a deep breath like I hadn't been able to breathe for a long time. When the lights came on the girl had disappeared and there was silence among the men for a minute like the silence that comes at eleven o'clock on November the eleventh. Then there was talking again and the bar tenders were throwing ice cubes in glasses and the room was back in the Chicago of 1959.

"How did you like her?" Danny asked me.

"Is her sister like that?"

"I don't know. Never met her."

Danny relighted his cigar and I ground mine out on the floor.

"Come on back to my office and we'll meet her sister."

As we picked our way through the crowd to the back room Danny told the M. C. to send Fran and her sister to the office.

Fran had on her green evening dress again and it seemed strange to see her dressed because she looked about like any other show girl with her clothes on, only her face was still a little flushed and her eyes were puffy like she had been making love.

"This is Mike. Remember I was telling you he'd take Ruth out? Mike meet Fran."

"I liked your show."

"Then you're O. K. with me." She shook hands with me.

"Where's your sister?" Danny asked.

"She was lying down. I'll go back and see if she's finished putting on her face."

"Not bad?" Danny said when she had gone.

"She's a lot of woman."

I soon found out that her sister was very different. She was young, certainly not over sixteen, and it was her first trip away from home. She looked like just another scared kid who was getting into something she didn't understand. She was tall and so young that she wasn't really filled out yet and when I saw her I wondered why Danny hadn't gotten a date with her himself. I guess he didn't know how young she was going to be.

Danny whispered something to Fran. Fran laughed and said, "Of course not" and put her arm around her little sister.

As we left the strip joint Danny kept looking at my date like he wished he had met her first.

CHAPTER FIVE

W E WRAPPED the town up fine that night. I really felt like somebody driving up to the door with Danny and the girls in that cream colored Caddy and having door men all but bow as they helped us out.

First we went down to the Loop and caught an ice show at the Boulevard Room and then we went to Barney's for a steak. After that Danny said he wanted to show us how the other half lived and took us to the Buttery at the Ambassador West.

Sitting there watching the college kids drink I got to thinking about Kitty. She was like those college kids, clean and well groomed. It was funny to see how different they were from our dates. They could be wearing the same clothes and eating the same food, but there was a difference that you could always spot. I was sure those college kids raised their bits of hell and that one or two of the girls there had probably had as much experience as Fran, but there was a difference and it made me feel big as hell to know Kitty and I wished she'd hurry back.

While I was sitting there drinking I got to thinking about her husband with the stinking ulcer on his leg. I could picture him doing all kinds of dirty things to her. I had to drink a lot just to sit still.

We were all drinking heavy except Ruth. She just sat there and tried to take it all in without staring. When she took a sip of her drink I could tell she wasn't used to drinking and that she didn't like it. Studying her helped me get my mind off Kitty and I began to wonder why she came to Chicago to live with a sister like Fran. Somehow you'd picture Ruth going to a country schoolhouse some place and then marrying the farmer's son and having a dozen kids and growing old without ever going to a strip joint in Chicago. Later I learned that she hadn't wanted to come to Chicago at all. She had lived with her father on a farm in down state Illinois. Three months before she came to Chicago her father had had a stroke. She took care of him there at home until the doctor told him he would never be able to farm again. He sold the place and went to live with his brother in Davenport. There wasn't room for Ruth too, so it was decided that she should come to Chicago and stay with her older sister. I guess the others in the family thought Fran was acting in plays when she told them she was on the stage.

"Did you see your sister's act tonight?" I asked Ruth when the others got up to dance.

"No."

She looked down at her glass and I could tell she was embarrassed.

"She's quite a girl."

"I didn't know she worked in a place like that."

"Would you have come to live with her if you had known?"

"I guess so. I didn't have much choice," she said and then told me about her father's sickness.

"You going to work there too?"

"Fran said I'd have to. I don't know how to do office work or anything like that."

"Can you dance?"

"No, but Fran said she'd teach me."

"I'll bet she'll teach you lots of things."

"I'm pretty green about everything, but Fran told me what to do. I'll get along."

"You'd better be careful or your sister'll get you in trouble."

And as I was saying this I wondered why I should be warning her. After all she was my date and I had every intention of getting her in as much trouble as possible before the night was over. The kind of get togethers Danny gave weren't exactly tea parties. Danny liked to start off by hitting the town and drinking enough to mellow up. Then he liked to take everybody to his place and really get stinko.

Danny came back to the table puffing and laughing as he sat down without holding the chair for Fran.

"Why don't you two love birds give it a fling?"

"Would you like to dance?" I asked Ruth.

"I'm not very good."

"Go on, give it a try," Fran said and Ruth stood up like she had made up her mind to do everything just like her sister said.

Ruth was right. She wasn't a good dancer. She followed me all right, but she was stiff and frightened and I knew she wouldn't be able to get up on that stage where Fran worked and give much of a freewheeling demonstration and besides that she didn't have much to demonstrate. She was so young that her figure wasn't filled out yet. Her hips were like a boy's and her hard little breasts weren't as large as golf balls. I felt sorry as hell for her, but I guessed she had already been initiated and was well on the road to becoming like her sister.

She was glad to sit down when the music stopped.

"You'll feel a lot better if you get some drinks in you," I whispered to her as we were walking back to the table. "It would help you relax."

She nodded and smiled weakly. When we sat down again I ordered a double whiskey for Ruth. She looked at me with her big deer eyes and then drank it all down without taking a breath.

"Look at that girl go. You're getting the spirit now," Danny said and laughed as he told the waiter to give them all another double.

By the time we were at Danny's apartment Ruth was so wobbly I had to help her out of the car. I put my arm way around her slim chest so I could feel the edge of her hard little breasts and suddenly I wanted to go upstairs right away and get down to business, only this time Danny wasn't going to have the kind of fancy switch parties he liked.

"Now we'll have a real party," Danny said when we got inside his five-hundred-a-month apartment that overlooked the lake. "You girls can take off your things while I get the whiskey."

I looked around the living room at the fancy modernistic furniture. When he came back with a couple of bottles I was standing in front of the picture window that looked out over the lake twenty stories below.

"That dame of yours is gonna be all right," he said and slapped me on the back.

"She's too young for this kind of party."

"Awe, come off of it, Mike, I thought you wanted to have a real party. We'll get the girls a little more liquored up and then let Fran give her sister a lesson in stripping.

Danny was right, I had set my heart on a real party that night, but now that I had been around Ruth for a few hours I changed my mind. She was just a sweet corn fed girl from Nowhere U. S. A. and I didn't want to be the one to introduce her to a big city life like Danny knew. Well, I might not be able to talk Danny out of a big party, but I would certainly keep him away from Ruth even if I ended up slugging it out with him.

"Let's have a couple of shots while the girls are straightening up," I said to Danny. If I could get him drunk enough maybe my job would be a good deal easier. Then I remembered Danny kept some knock out drops around the apartment someplace to use on girls if they really wanted to hold out on him. I decided to have a look for the medicine and try to slip some in Danny's drink. Would he ever hate me in the morning if he ever found out what I did to him!

"What else do you have around as a mix?" I asked.

"About everything you ever heard of, old pal. You name it and Danny has it."

"I'd like to have some cream to make a King Alphonso."

"A what?" he said like I had told him I wanted the S. S. Queen Mary to float in my bathtub.

"I want a King Alphonso. Didn't you ever hear of that?"

"Sure, but I never heard of anybody drinking it on a party."

"Then you've heard of something new tonight," I said. "O. K. if I go back in the kitchen for some cream?"

"I'll get it for you. Nothing's too good tonight for my friend Mike Callahan."

After Danny left the room I quickly searched the liquor cabinet for the chloral drops. I couldn't find any there or in the dining room cupboard. Danny came back just as I seated myself in the living room again.

"Here's a King Alphonso for my good friend Mike Callahan."

"Thanks, Danny," I said and took a sip of the sweet drink. He was right, it was a mighty poor drink to have on a party and my stomach objected to mixing it with the bourbon highballs that had gone before, but I had asked for it and now I had to drink it. The girls came back in the room as we sat there nursing along our drinks. Fran went over to sit on Danny's knee and Ruth sat down on the sofa beside me.

"Do you feel better now?" I asked her. She nodded her head and looked up at me with her big sky eyes. No, I wasn't going to let anything happen to her. I felt very tender towards her and I was sorry that she had come to Chicago. It was times like that, that I wished I knew something about life, why the whole world was so screwed up, why you felt good one minute and bad the next and what was right and what was wrong. I wish I was one of those smart college guys that knew all about everything and for a minute I even thought about going to night school so I could get all the answers like that college guy I had known in the army. But then I wondered if those college guys knew it all. This college guy I had known in the army had ended up by putting a M1 rifle in his mouth and blowing the top of his head off. But maybe that was because he was so smart. Maybe that was the real answer.

When I finished my drink I told Danny that I was going in the kitchen to get my own cream this time. He was busy turning off the lights and didn't say "no." I looked through the refrigerator and kitchen cabinets for the chloral, but I wasn't able to find any. While I was mixing my drink there in the kitchen I heard Danny call me.

"Come on back and see the show."

When I got in the living room I found he had put out all the lights except one which he had propped against a chair and pointed at the two girls who stood in the middle of the room. Ella Fitzgerald was giving with some sexy music over the hi-fi in the corner.

"Now show her how to strip," Danny said.

Ruth was frightened. Her big sister was standing there big as hell with her legs spread apart slowly throwing her hips around in a circle.

"You start like this," she was telling her sister.

"Fran, please, I can't do it."

"Go on. Have a try at it."

Ruth tried, but there was no freedom in her movement. She didn't know enough about life to know what she was supposed to be imitating.

"And like this," Fran said and gave some bumps. Now she was getting into it with her whole body. She undid her zipper down the front so that you could get a good look at her twirling assets.

"Damn you, try," Danny shouted at the other girl.

"Please, I can't do it."

Danny walked over to her, grabbed a handful of her dress and ripped it down to her waist.

"Damn it try or I'll beat you so blue you'll think a train hit you."

"Take it easy, Danny," I said. I didn't want to fight him because he had the kind of friends that could hit back, but if he pushed me far enough I would keep him off Ruth.

You had to hand it to the poor kid. She did try even though she was scared to death. Her dancing was more a tremble than a wiggle.

"Now take the rest of it off and let's see your merchandise," he shouted and finished the glass of bourbon in his hand.

"Please, I can't do it."

He got up from where he was sitting and staggered over toward her.

He put his hand down in her dress and pinched her.

She screamed.

That was when I hit him. For a minute his eyes went open wide like he didn't believe it and then he charged into me and started throwing wild punches at my face, but they weren't all wild because one of them knocked me down and in a second he was on top of me. We went rolling over and over and then he jumped up and the next thing I knew a metal ash tray glanced off my head and struck the floor by my right ear. I rolled over and was able to get my arms around his legs and pull him down on the floor beside me. I crawled on top and smashed him in the jaw with my fist. I could feel his jaw turn to mush under the blow and I knew the fight was over. He just groaned and held both hands against his jaw like it would come off if he let go.

"Put on your things, we're getting out of here," I said to Ruth.

She dressed and we left while Fran was still putting cold wet towels on Danny's face.

CHAPTER SIX

W HEN Ruth and I reached the street below there was a soft warm early morning breeze coming in from the lake and you could tell from the pearl grey color of the sky out over the lake that it was nearly morning.

I didn't know what to do with Ruth. Now I had taken her away from her sister so it was up to me to take care of her.

I reached down and took her hand in mine and without speaking we walked to the underpass at Michigan and Oak and went down the steps and through the dark tunnel over to the beach. We walked on up the beach a little way and sat down to rest. I put my arm around her slender shoulders and she let her head relax on my arm like she was trusting me to help her.

We sat there for a long time without talking, looking out over the water that was still and grey, letting the warm breeze rumple our hair.

After a while I began talking softly.

"Ruth, you got yourself in a mess by coming to Chicago."

I waited for her to agree with me, but she didn't say anything. I looked down at her face to see if she was asleep, but she wasn't. I guess she was just too done in by everything to talk about it.

"I don't care how tough things are with you, you can't go back with your sister. She's bad all the way through. Maybe it's not all her fault but she's not much better than a prostitute and if you stay around her you'll get the same way."

I stopped for a minute trying to think of what to say next, but I wasn't much good at preaching.

'I've knocked around the world a lot and I know some things you couldn't possibly know. I know how girls like your sister end up. Life's a lot of hell raising fun for her now, but in five more years her body will be too old for a stripper and Danny or somebody like him will fire her and then she'll start rustling for sure and she won't be a first class one either. There'll be lines on her face and dark circles under her eyes from the kind of life she's led and she won't be able to even a get a good price for selling herself and then she'll drink more and pretty soon any drunk will be able to have her for only a couple of shots of bar whiskey. Then she'll drink more and more to kill all the hate in her that she'll feel and then she'll get a bad liver or she'll go on dope or she'll get pneumonia some cold night lying in a dark alley where some guy will leave her after knocking her in the head and they'll take her to County Hospital where she'll die and be buried in an unmarked grave.

"And if you start now, something will be killed inside you and you'll go the same way. Do you know that?"

"Yes."

"I'm afraid. I don't know anybody in Chicago and I don't know how to get a job or a place to live or anything. And I can't go back home. I don't have any home."

It seemed screwy that a girl should feel so lost in a place like Chicago and then I tried to think back to when I was her age. I remembered that the world seemed very complicated and strange to me then. If I had come to Chicago from a farm where I had lived a quiet life with my family, I guess Chicago would have been even larger. She didn't know about things like Traveler's Aid or the Y.W.C.A. or night school or employment agencies. They were all things of the city that she had never even heard of. She knew as little about them as I knew of the 4H clubs.

Talking with Ruth and sitting there with my arm around her made me feel like a better man. Here was someone who trusted me enough to leave her own sister and go out into the city with me alone.

I wasn't in love with her or anything but I felt very tender. It must be the same feeling a mother has when she puts her arm around her small child that is so defenseless and that trusts her for food and protection.

I squeezed her thin shoulder with my hand and I wanted to say foolish things that I had never said before. I wanted to say, "There, there I'll take care of you. Everything will be all right"

For the first time in my life I wasn't just out to get all I could from the world. It was a good feeling and I wished it would last, but I was sure it would go away when it got light and I would be the same as always. You don't turn soft that easy.

We sat there a long time with her head on my shoulder and my arm around her. When we got up to leave the sun was coming up out of the lake and the cars were beginning to swish past on the Outer Drive behind us.

"I think the Y.W.C.A. would be the best place for you to stay."

"Can I go back to our hotel for my things?"

"Do you have a key to the room?"

"No."

"Then let's skip it."

"But I've got to have some clothes to wear."

"You aren't just trying to find an excuse to go back with your sister?"

I had seen lots of girls who would really like to be strippers. For all I knew that was what Ruth really wanted. She had never said much about really wanting to leave her sister.

"No, it's not that. I've just got to have some clothes to wear."

"You're sure you want to leave your sister for good?"

"Yes."

"Then I'll go with you to the hotel and see to it that there's no trouble."

As we walked back through the underpass I was thinking about what a crazy mess I was in. Here a rough guy like me had just talked a kid into leaving her sister so she could get started on the right road. What would Fran do if she found out that I got her sister into leaving? I wondered if she could have me put in jail.

We stopped at an all night coffee shop on the Near North Side for breakfast and then walked on over to Fran's hotel on Delaware Street. There was no key downstairs in the mail slot, but I gave the night clerk five dollars and that was enough to convince the old man that our purposes for entering the room were strictly honorable.

She didn't have many clothes. There were some sweaters and skirts and a pair of battered saddle shoes. There wasn't much she could wear to look for a job in Chicago.

As we left the building I told the night man not to say anything about our visit.

"I'd get fired if I did," he said and settled back down to sleep in the overstuffed chair in the lobby.

On the way to the McCormick Y.W.C.A. on Dearborn Street I told Ruth that there were agencies in the city to take care of girls like her.

"They'll see to it that you get a job."

"It's awful nice of you to help me like this."

"Here take this," I said, giving her two twenty dollar bills, "you'll need something for your first week's rent and use the rest to buy some clothes with. Tomorrow morning find out who's in charge of this place and ask her what kind of clothes to buy and where you can buy them the cheapest."

"I've got enough clothes to last awhile."

"Those clothes you have are O.K. for high school kids, but as of today you're a career girl and they won't do for that."

"I'll pay you back sometime."

"Forget it."

As we stood on the steps of the "Y" I told her to be sure that she got in touch with the woman in charge and did like she said. I gave her the pressed-paper suitcase and watched as she went up the steps and through the front door.

I didn't feel like going to bed, so I took a street car down to the loop and wandered around for awhile trying to find something to do to pass the time. At last I settled for a movie.

By the time the movie was over I was sleepy. I walked out of the theater into the hot air that was already taking the city over for the day. It wouldn't be much of an afternoon to catch up on sleep, even in my room near the lake.

I got off the Sheridan Avenue bus in front of the house and noticed two men in a black heap parked across the street. At the time I didn't think anything of it and walked on down the drive carrying my coat over my shoulder. I went up the outside stairs to my room over the garage and threw open the windows to let in some air. As I was taking off my shirt I turned around and saw two big bruisers standing in the door. They looked like something that had escaped from the Museum of Natural History.

"You Mike Callahan?" the one in front asked.

"That's right."

"Danny wants to know where you took Fran's sister."

"Tell him to look her up in the phone directory."

"Smart guy."

"I almost finished high school."

"Come on Little Willie," he said to the man behind him and they pushed into the room.

I looked around for something to bash their brains out with and came up with a metal lamp that stood on the table by the bed. Maybe they would give me a beating, but they wouldn't come out of it without a few scratches.

"What's holding you?" I stood holding the lamp, waiting for them to get tough.

They knew I wasn't any push over like the little guys they were used to beating up for half a C note.

"Come on you bull necked bastards." I might just as well have some fun. Either way I was going to get a beating. There's nothing these big bruisers hate more than to be called a fairy.

"Which one of you guys acts like the girl when you make love?"

When I said that Little Willie started to charge me, but the other guy held him back.

"We got to get the info first," he said.

"I'm gonna kill him."

"Come on tell us what you did with the girl. You just as well tell us now, because you know damn well you'll tell us before we're through with you."

"I got her chained under my bed."

Little Willie was ready to look under the bed when the other guy stopped him. The smart one must have taken a correspondence course at Leavenworth.

"This is the last time I'm gonna ask you."

"Ask me what?"

"It's the last time I'm gonna ask you what you did with the girl."

"What do you mean?"

"You know what I mean. Where did you leave her?"

"On the steps."

"What steps?"

"I forget."

They started on in the room, Little Willie going to the right and the other big bruiser coming in on the left. I held the lamp tight in my hand and moved back a little towards the wall so they couldn't get behind me. Little Willie was the first to come in close. He kept edging towards me and then all of a sudden he rushed me. I hit him square on the side of the head with the brass lamp and he went down for the count. Before I could get my balance again the other guy was all over me and the lamp wasn't much good. He tried to get a hammer lock on my head, but I slipped out of his arm and ran over to the other side of the room. Now Little Willie was sitting on the floor feeling his head and wearing a silly look on his ape face.

"Come on over and I'll give it to you," I said. I'm one hell of a big man myself and there aren't many who'll rush me one at a time, but this one was so dumb he charged right in again. I hit him on the head and the lamp glanced off like it had struck a rock. His fist hit me in the chest and I was thrown back against the wall and then he was mugging me again. I got a good right on his chin as he was trying to get a grip on my head again and then I felt something around my legs and knew Little Willie was back in circulation. I kicked him in the face and cracked my heel across the back of his hand. It didn't knock him cold; nothing short of that would stop him. He got both arms around my legs and I went down on the floor. But I was the only one there. The other two guys got up quick and began kicking me. I guess that was their special method because they were good and thorough about it. When I lunged for one of their feet the other one would kick me in the chest so I would pull my arm back in and try to protect myself. After that went on a couple of seconds I got frightened and bloody and there's nothing stronger than a man who's mad and tasting blood. I lunged up at Little Willie and somehow got him down on the floor with me. I could feel the other guy kicking me but I didn't give a damn. I was going to get one of them. I caught Little Willie's arm and turned him over on his face. When I forced his arm up behind his back I wasn't gentle about it. I didn't do it by degrees and ask him if he had had enough. I just forced his aim up till it got hard to push and then I gave a big heave and felt the arm go limp as the bone cracked. He screamed bloody murder and the kicks kept raining down on me from above. A shoe hit me in the temple and for a second I didn't know where I was. After that there wasn't much fight left in me. The last thing I remember was a kick in the groin with a size fourteen shoe while I was trying to cover my face. That kick did it. The whole sky looked like the Milky Way and there were about six too many moons in the room. I turned over, retched on the floor and passed the hell out.

CHAPTER SEVEN

PRETTY soon I opened my eyes enough to see the room spinning around me and feel the pulsating ache where I had been kicked. When I tried to move the pain went down my legs like electric shocks and I threw up again. I must have passed out because the next thing I knew the early afternoon sun was shining down on my face from the west side window. This time I was able to pull myself to the bed and telephone for somebody in the house to come out and help me. I told them to send anybody except Karl, but Karl was the one who came.

"First you make love to Mrs. Grey and now you get mixed up with a bunch of thugs," he said, looking down at me where I lay stretched out on top of the bed.

It hurt too much to move and he had to cut my clothes off. When I was finally undressed I looked down to see what they had done to me. There was not a two inch spot on my body that had missed being kicked black.

"We'll have to take you to a hospital," Karl said.

I'm sure he hated to lose such a good source of labor, but there wasn't much else he could do about it. He called an ambulance and they took me to Memorial Hospital. The next twenty-four hours weren't so bad because they kept me so doped up with hypos that I didn't even know who I was. Every few hours I would look up to see a pretty nurse sticking a needle in my arm or an intern starting another bottle of fluid in my vein.

I remember the police asking me what happened. I told them two thugs tried to make me give them information about the location of the family silver. I don't know how I managed to stick to my story with all the dope they gave me, but I did. There wasn't much use in telling them about Danny and Ruth. Fellows like that always have a cop or two they're paying off for protection and he could buy a hundred men who would swear they had been playing poker with him all night.

But Karl didn't believe my story. You'll have to give him credit for being the smartest one around. Of course the whole thing was fishy. Who ever heard of a couple of robbers operating that way? If I'd been in my right mind I could have made up a lot better tale.

But I decided on a story and stuck to it without any variations and the rest of them believed me before it was all over.

I didn't know I was any kind of hero until the supervisor of nurses told me one day. Miss Watson was a woman about fifty years old with grey hair and a large bosom. Every day she would go around to see the seriously ill patients and I had come to enjoy my talks with her. She was a little on the holy side and was always preaching to me. "The Man upstairs is watching over us," she would often say.

"Mr. Grey is arranging to give you a reward," she told me after settling herself in a chair by the window one morning. Then she went on telling me about how long she had known David Grey and what a fine man he was. After recovering from the coma he had donated a few grand to the hospital for a new laundry machine and in her eyes that made him a fine man. I wondered what she would say if I told her about the things he made his young wife do in bed.

"I understand Mrs. Grey (meaning Kitty) was a student nurse here when they were married."

"She was a student here when she met him, but she had stopped her training before they were married."

"What made her give up nursing?"

"I would rather not talk about that if you don't mind, Mr. Callahan," she said and then she left the room before I had time to question her anymore about the reason for Kitty leaving. I wondered why she avoided the question. After she left the room I tried to think of reasons why student nurses would stop their training program. Maybe some of them found it dull or too hard or too bloody. But none of these reasons would fit Kitty. She was certainly not the type to be frightened by the sight of a little blood. Maybe she was sure she could marry David and didn't see much point in staying on the bedpan detail any longer.

I forgot about the whole thing and went to sleep.

The next morning the old hunchbacked male nurse named Glen was giving me my bath when I got to wondering about Kitty again.

"Glen, did you ever know Kitty Phillips when she was a student nurse here?"

'You mean Mrs. Grey?"

"That's right."

"Sure I remember her. You don't forget a face like hers."

"How long did she stop her job here before she married Mr. Grey?"

"Oh, I'd say she quit here about six months before she was married."

I turned over for him to wash my back and he went on.

"You can't exactly say she quit."

"What do you mean?"

"This is just between you and me."

"Sure thing."

"She was asked to quit."

"What did she do?"

"Nothing was ever proved. It was all hushed up and I don't know exactly why she had to leave. There were lots of tales going around. Some say she stayed out too late one night and others say she shot off her mouth to Miss Watson. I don't rightly know just what did happen."

I asked him some more questions about it, but he didn't know anymore. I made up my mind to ask Kitty the next time I saw her. I was sure there was something funny about it because Miss Watson never did come back for any of her friendly chats after that. She would just stick her head in the door long enough to say hello and leave before I had time to ask her any questions.

The x-ray showed that I didn't have anything broken except three ribs. After about a week my left side went down to its usual size and I got out of bed. I was still sore all right but it wasn't the same kind of sharp pain that I had had at first. Now I just felt like a man about ninety years old.

I was tired as hell after sitting up for twenty minutes. When I climbed back in bed and lay still waiting for supper I got to thinking about my future. I did that every now and then and it always made me get the blues. I knew I didn't have any future. I would always be just a plain jerk who did stinking little things like chauffeuring for a living. I wouldn't ever save any lives or climb any mountains or make any inventions.

But still I got to thinking every new and then. There was something in me somewhere that still had crazy dreams. That something in me wouldn't believe me when I told it that I would always be a tramp and that afternoon something in me that would not be discouraged by the truth got to bothering me.

I thought about the big deal I had lined up on the coast just to see it fall flat. Then I remembered how I had felt when I got back to Chicago. I was going to give driving lessons for a few weeks while I lined up another good deal, but instead I took a job chauffeuring to be around a skirt that had run out on me after a month. I could have worked out something with that bum Danny but now he'd have every sharpie in the city down on me. Anyway, I wanted to go legitimate this time.

I just lay there between the smooth white sheets waiting for supper trying to think of someway I could make a decent living and all of a sudden it came to me: I would open a hash house somewhere. My old lady had run a combination tavern-restaurant (those are mighty kind words for the dump she ran over on West Madison Street) and I had learned something about the business when I was a kid. It was the only legitimate business besides soldiering that I knew a damn thing about.

Suddenly I could see it all there in front of me. I could see a little hash house somewhere on the North side that would start out as a two-by-four room with burgers and beer and I could see it grow into a respectable place like Isabelle's where you could buy quail and roast venison. I could save enough out of my pay to get started and then I could nurse it along and see that it grew into something I wanted.

When I got through the dream I told myself that it was all just a lot of hot air and that I'd always be a jerk, but that little bastard inside of me didn't believe what I told it. It said "Go on and think about it. What you got to lose except your reputation as a jerk?"

I was lying there on the bed with my eyes closed thinking about the restaurant deal when I heard someone walk up to the bed. I thought it was one of the nurses coming to take my afternoon temperature. I rolled over and saw Kitty.

She was standing there alone by my bed smiling down at me. You never saw anybody look so pretty. She had a new sun tan and her hair had been bleached even blonder by the sun. She was wearing a freshly starched blue linen dress and she had that smooth, well-groomed look about her that only rich people ever have. Christ how could I ever fool myself into thinking a gal like that could care about a jerk like me?

"I have a reward for you," she said smiling down at me.

"What for?"

"For saving the house."

"Forget it."

"No, I'm serious. David wants you to have a reward."

She opened her purse and handed me a check for a thousand dollars. My hash house looked pretty real right then.

"And I have my own personal reward."

She went to the door and gently closed it. She came back and smiled down at me before bending over and planting a big red kiss right on my forehead.

"You can do better than that."

"Is this better?"

She kissed me on the lips this time. My arms went around her and pulled her against me so I could feel her hard breasts against my chest.

"That's better."

"It's good to see you again, Mike."

She rested her head against my shoulder while my hand made circling movements over her.

"Did you miss me?"

"More than I like to admit."

"Give me another one of those kisses."

This time she leaned down and kissed me like she meant it. The hospital room was no place for us to get to feeling this way about each other, but two weeks was a long time for hot blooded people like us. The old flood gate opened up again and before we knew it we were pushing against each other hard enough to make my broken ribs feel like hot pins in my chest, but I didn't tell her to stop. The pain would go away.

Her tongue did little things to me that made my hair stand on end. My hands were all over her and we were moaning again. She had missed me alright.

"Baby, you got it. You got all of it."

"Hummm," she said and kept right on doing the devilish things you shouldn't do to a sick man.

"Come on. Crawl in bed with me."

"Darling not here. I can't here."

But she pushed against me and did everything it was possible to do without taking off our clothes. Then suddenly her whole body began jerking. It was the first time I ever heard of it happening to a girl when she was doing nothing but kissing, but then there weren't any more girls like Kitty, not in my life, not in anybody's life.

She knelt down on the floor and rested her head on the bed beside me as she waited for her strength to come back. At last she was back in this world again.

"Are we going to have some more fun when I get out of this rat trap?"

"Sure. I've got it all planned out."

"Let's hear it."

"When you get out of the hospital I'll have them take you to our summer place on Lake Geneva."

"David wouldn't do that."

"Certainly he would. You're a hero. You were almost killed protecting his property. There's nothing too good for you."

"And what if I do get farmed out up there?"

"I'll spend the summer with you."

"Just you?"

"Oh, we'll have a cook and a maid come along."

'What about David?"

"He doesn't like it up there. Believe me we'll have a beautiful summer."

"I believe you."

"You'd better wipe off the lipstick. Here I'll do it for you."

"Where's your ring?" I asked when I saw she was not wearing it.

"Left it home when I went to Hot Springs."

Then she told me all about her trip, about the plane trip and the hot baths they gave at the resort and how all the dowdy old people sat around on the hotel porch talking about the things they used to do. She said that she had missed me more than she liked to admit.

"But the tennis instructor wasn't old."

"Did you improve your game?"

"Certainly."

She laughed because she could see I was jealous.

"And you stuck to tennis all the time?"

"Nothing but tennis. Why, would you have minded?"

"You know damn well I would have minded."

"Don't worry, if I have a baby it'll be yours."

I turned and looked at her.

"I said *if.*"

"Don't scare me that way."

"Does it scare you to have a baby?"

"Yes. I couldn't stand it. Why any man that loves a woman wants her to have babies seems queer to me. I couldn't stand seeing your middle puff up till you looked like you'd swallowed a watermelon."

The nurse knocked on the door and brought in my supper tray. She put it down on the bed and then rolled me up before leaving the room.

"I've got to be going," Kitty said.

"One more kiss first."

"All right."

And then after a minute:

"How was that?"

"That was one of the things I missed. We're going to have fun when you get out of here," she said and blew me a kiss as she said goodby and left the room.

CHAPTER EIGHT

I FELT BAD about taking the reward money, but I couldn't change my story and after all I had saved somebody in a way. I had saved Ruth from Danny.

Before I left the hospital for Lake Geneva I decided to give some of the money to Ruth so she would have a better chance to get started on the right track. I telephoned the McCormick Y.W.C.A. But they didn't have anybody by that name registered there. I asked them if she had been there and moved, but they just played dumb and said they had no record at all of a Ruth Sims.

That was a hell of a note, I thought, getting beat up like that for a girl you were going to save until then finding out that she didn't stay saved for even one day. That was a woman for you. A man my age should have had more sense about women, but some men never learned.

By the time I left the hospital to go to Lake Geneva I had forgotten all about Ruth. She was just another dame I had met in the night and known well for a few hours and left forever when the sun came up. Ruth wasn't like Kitty. You could forget the run-of- the-mill kind like Ruth.

Chicago was hot as a Bagdad laundry the day Kitty and I left for the lake. You could feel the heat coming down from the sky and you could feel it coming up from the pavement and coming at you from all sides as it was reflected off the buildings.

I mopped my face with a handkerchief as I went down the hospital steps with Kitty.

"And now it's your turn to be the chauffeur," I joked when I saw she had come for me in the station wagon.

"And you're the honored guest."

"And so forth."

"Check, and so forth."

"You're sure David's not going to be there?"

"He's afraid to get that far away from a doctor."

"Won't he be slightly suspicious when he thinks about us being up there all alone?"

"He heard you were seriously injured. Maybe he thinks you'll be incapacitated for a while."

"Maybe I will."

"I'm a good nurse."

"Meaning you'll cure me?"

"That's right."

"You'll probably kill me but I can't think of a nicer way to die."

As she drove out Foster Avenue I leaned back and rolled down the window in the back seat.

"It's too hot to do anything today."

"Wait till we get to the lake."

"Is the cottage in a quiet place?"

"Nothing but trees and our own private beach."

"Who takes care of the place?"

"We have an old man and his wife. They have a separate cottage about a quarter of a mile away."

"Then we'll have the house to ourselves at night?"

"That's right."

"Oh, brother, now I know why I didn't die."

As we left the crowded city and sped over the flat open highway it grew cooler.

After we were out of town ten or fifteen miles we stopped at a drive in for a cold bottle of beer. We just sat there in the car sipping the cold beer and smiling at each other. It was like we were two kids running away together to discover for the first time what love was like. I knew it was wrong for me to be going off like that with another man's wife, but then there was something right about it too. We were both young and we had such a big yen for each other and it was like owning each other was the only thing we had in the world, and everyone was due to have at least one thing in the world. David had his money and his position. He had a fine mansion on Sheridan Road and a limousine to drive around in, but we had love and right then I felt like the richest guy in the world. I was glad she had missed me while out of town.

We drank another bottle of beer and then Kitty started the car again. I liked the way she drove. It was like everything else she did—full of Kitty. She put the gear in first and started off so fast that the tires screamed and then she threw it into second and held it there till we were hitting about fifty. She was some woman. I'd known my share but I'd never known one with a spirit like hers, as wild and clean and unconquered as a summer storm.

We drove on north over the Illinois state line and into Wisconsin where the country side looked like real country with rolling hills and creeks and cows and mail boxes beside the road.

As we got near Lake Geneva we kept passing cars filled with people going up for a weekend of rest from the heat of Chicago. The people were laughing and driving crazy and sometimes you could see a bottle that was passing back and forth. It was the first vacation I'd ever had but I was getting the spirit of things already.

The "cottage" turned out to be a ten-room house with a big rustic living room made up like a hunting lodge with mounted animals on one wall. Out front there was a wide porch and past that was a neat lawn that ran down to the private beach and land-ing pier.

Mrs. Hobson, the caretaker's wife, was a buxom old lady who almost bowed when she spoke to you. After Kitty introduced me she told her that she could have the rest of the day off.

I knew why.

I put my suitcase down in the living room and followed Kitty into the bedroom.

"It's been a long time," I said and stood there running my fingers through her fine blonde hair, wanting to make it all last a long time because it was all so good, like a kid with a sucker that only licks now and then so it'll last all day.

"Mike, I'm going to ask something big of you."

Women and their ideas, I thought. Why didn't God make them without tongues and brains?

"All right."

"Mike, you know I'm very fond of you."

"I had an idea."

"Then you'll know it hurts me to say this."

"Let's have it."

Why did they always want a man to grovel in the dirt at their feet and beg them?

"Mike, I want you to promise me you won't try anything."

"Don't you want me?"

"Of course I want you. All the time we were gone I kept thinking about you and wanting you and remembering the times we had been together. Sure I want you."

"Here I am."

"I can't have you."

"Yes you can."

"Something inside me keeps me away. It won't let me have you like I want you."

"Then let's get drunk and put that something to sleep."

"But later it'll wake up and then I'll remember and everything will be all mixed up and I'll hate myself."

"Every person's got a right to love."

"But not me."

"Why?"

"You know why."

"David?"

"Yes."

"Then leave him. Divorce him and marry me."

"He'd never give me a divorce."

"Then leave him. We'll go away someplace together. I'll use the money to open up a hash house and we'll nurse it along till it turns into something big and then everything'll work out all right for both of us. You just need to get away from him."

We were sitting on the bed. I pushed down very gently and kissed her wide lips and put my arm around her to pull her against me.

"Let's run away together."

"I want to," she said and I started kissing her again.

"Do you like to be kissed this way?"

"No, not now. Be gentle. Kiss me with little kisses and hold my lips against yours and drink out of my lips and do it easy and tell me you love me."

"Baby I do love you."

"But don't say 'baby.' "

"What should I say?"

"Be gentle."

"Kitty, Katherine, I love you. I have a heart and I love you with all of it."

"That's the way."

I pulled her body over against me, gently. I moved my hand up and down her thigh, gently, so gently it was torture.

"And is that the way?"

"Oh, yes."

"My little Kitty," I said as I restrained my lips and made them play with her. It was wonderful. I had never made love this way before. Kitty was the one I had been looking for when I was with all those other girls. No wonder they hadn't worked out right. She was the end. The greatest.

"Now kiss me a little harder."

And after a minute:

"No, not that hard."

But I couldn't stand it any longer. I pulled her body against mine and crushed my lips on hers.

"Mike, it's not right!"

She leaped up from the bed and ran into the bathroom and locked the door. I could hear the water running and every now and then I could hear her crying.

She wanted to make love as bad as I did. The poor kid was all mixed up inside. It's hell to be thirty but it's even more hell to be twenty-two and not know what the world's about. And anyway you look at it, it's more hell to be a woman. They get the short end of every deal in the world.

Pretty soon she came out. She didn't look fresh and well groomed and rich and happy any longer. She looked all wilted up inside. Her eyes were red from crying and her dress was all wrinkled and her long blonde hair needed brushing a thousand times.

"I'm sorry, kid."

She came over to where I sat on the bed and kneeled down beside me and looked up at me like a little puppy dog.

"I'm sorry, kid."

I sat there for a long time running my hand through her hair and thinking about what a stinking world it was. You never got what you really wanted. But then you never stopped trying because when you stopped trying you were dead.

"You really love me, don't you, kid?"

"Yes, Mike. I never knew what it was till I met you. That first day when I let you make love to me I'm sure you thought I was just a rich tramp, but I wasn't. I was all dead inside and tied in knots and I had to have you untie the knots and make everything right again."

"And now everything's all tied in knots again?"

"Yes, everything's all tied in knots again."

"Let's run away together."

"We've got to do something."

"Then you'll leave with me?"

"I guess that's the best thing, Mike. Nothing we can do would be right, but if we ran away together at least it would be better because then I would only have one man."

"We can tell everybody that you're my wife."

"That would help."

"And I'd even buy you a wedding band."

"A plain gold one?"

"That's right, a plain gold one and I'd have our names put inside."

"And the date."

"What date?"

"The date we first met."

"It was wonderful."

"Yes."

"And soon we'll have each other like that all the time."

"That's what I want, Mike."

Then I took her arms and pulled her up on the bed with me. I didn't try again. I just put her head over on the pillow by mine where I could look in her eyes and touch my lips against hers. We didn't really kiss. We just made it so our lips touched and were wet together and we stayed there and talked with our lips touching all the time and we just lay there and looked at each other.

We went to sleep that way. Suddenly I was in a great black valley with great black clouds overhead. I was running like the wind and I went through a dark tunnel and when I came out on the other side I was a kid back in my mother's run-down tavern on West Madison Street. But mother wasn't old like I remembered her. She was like the picture she had that was taken when she was in high school. Her hair was long and light and hung down to her shoulders and her body was trim and young and her eyes were still full of dancing lights.

The music from the juke box was blaring and I stood in front of the box watching all the colored lights turning on and off. It was Saturday night and behind me the tavern was full of laughing people who were sitting at the bar drinking.

Suddenly everything was quiet.

An old man was standing in the center of the floor and my mother was walking towards him with her head bowed. When she came up to him he struck her in the face and then I was filled with sickness because the man and my mother were struggling on the floor and I was sure he was going to kill her.

I ran towards them to save my mother and suddenly as I ran there was a knife in my hand and I plunged the knife into the man's back and he rolled over to grab me and I cut his throat and the blood ran out of his neck on to the floor and he lay limp and I just stood there plunging the knife in him even though he was dead.

And then suddenly I was no longer a child. I was a middle aged man and I put an arm about my mother's waist and we walked out of the door together into the dark.

Then I was awake again and lying there in the bed with Kitty and for a second it seemed that she was the other woman.

"What's the matter?" she asked.

"Nothing. Just let me hold you tight."

"Yes."

"You won't ever leave me, Kitty?"

"Never."

"We'll work out something. I don't want to live without you, Kitty."

Everything seemed to change then. After the dream she seemed more a part of me and something that I could never leave.

CHAPTER NINE

WE HAD a week together up at the lake. We didn't make serious love. It was more like we were sweethearts romping around in the sun. In the mornings we'd go swimming and then fish for awhile or sail the sloop down to the village where we'd go shopping for groceries. One night we sailed over and went to the dance that was given so the bachelor boys and girls could meet each other.

All the laughing and playing together seemed to draw us even closer together. We began having our own jokes about people and soon we got to know each other well enough to say the intimate words that married people say to each other in fun.

Little things like that are what make two people married. They get to know all about each other and there's not a wall between them any more.

By the end of the week we had our escape plans all laid out. I was to cash the check and we would use it to buy a hash house someplace. She had a little money of her own in the bank and she would lend me that if we needed any more. She would write a note to David and we would just leave together without even saying anything about a divorce.

But we weren't going to leave Chicago. Chicago is such a big city that we could be lost from the rest of the world right there. No use going to Omaha or Salt Lake City.

On Saturday night our plans were suddenly changed. While we were eating supper and talking about the dance we were going to, a car drove up and parked outside the dining room window.

Karl was driving and David was sitting in the back seat.

"Here's the end of our picnic," I said.

I could see the disappointment come over her face.

"Damn him, I didn't think he'd ever come up here."

"Maybe he's suspicious. Karl saw you come down from my room one time when we were in town. Maybe he told David about it."

"You should have told me."

"What good would it have done?"

"I don't know."

We got up and went to the front door to meet them. David put his arm around her and kissed her lips.

"You look much better," he said, turning to me.

"Thanks, everything's healing."

I stood there and watched him as he kissed Kitty again. I hated that fat old man with the bald head. He limped on into the living room and lowered himself into a chair. Kitty got a stool and put it in front of the chair so he could use it to support his leg.

"How's the leg?" I asked.

"Much better. I think the trip did it good."

After we all had a drink he turned to me again.

"Would you like a job as my body guard?" he asked.

"That would be something new."

"You've been very good so far about protecting my property. My lawyer advised me to get a body guard and I thought of you right away. You're large enough to make any criminal think twice."

"Criminal?"

"That's right. I've had some trouble."

"What kind?"

"I found some of the boys were using the third floor of one of my hotels for book making and I put them out. The other day I received a threatening note."

"I'd like a month off before starting."

"That could be arranged. I'll hire a private detective in the mean time."

We didn't go to the dance that night. Instead we played canasta until I damn near had a hemorrhage from boredom.

That night I lay in my bed listening to David and Kitty going to bed. I knew there wouldn't be many more nights for me to suffer like that. I tossed on the bed and pulled the sheet this way and that until the bed looked like a tornado had slept there. I tried counting sheep and when that didn't work I went over the plans Kitty and I had talked about. It had all seemed very real when we were talking about it, but now that David was back I wondered if they would just be a bunch of dreams cooked up by a couple of moon-struck kids. At last I got up and sat in the chair by the window and smoked a cigarette. I wouldn't be able to take this every night. If David stayed I'd have to leave tomorrow. I wanted to go in the next room and smash his head in and take his wife away with me. No man can stand living with thoughts like that all the time.

After I finished smoking the fag I got a drink of water and went back to bed. It was the same story all over again. I tried counting sheep and then I made up a little game of going back and re-laying all the girls I'd layed. I got lost somewhere around number eighteen and gave that up.

There weren't but two things that could have put me to sleep that night, a woman or a drink. I went out to the kitchen to get a bottle and then decided it would be cooler out on the front porch.

As soon as I stepped out of the door I knew there was somebody else there. I thought about David's threatening letter and gripped the neck of the bottle to use it for a black jack.

"Is that you, Mike?"

"Kitty?"

"Yes."

I went down to the end of the porch where she sat.

"What are you doing out here?" I whispered.

"I couldn't stand him any longer."

I reached down to touch her. My hand felt her cheek and it was wet.

For the first time I felt real murder in my blood.

"What did he do?"

I had my arm around her and I could feel her shiver.

She buried her face against my shoulder and cried like a hurt kid. I stroked her hair and let her cry but I wasn't thinking nice thoughts. I was figuring out ways I could kill David and get away with it. I could kill him and then take his body out in the woods some place and bury him and if I buried him deep and did a good job of it they would never find the body. The police couldn't scream murder if they didn't have a body on their hands.

Then I thought about Karl. I'd have to kill him too. Well, that could be done.

Then I thought of the caretakers and then I knew I was thinking in crazy circles. I couldn't kill them all and expect to get away with it. A good murderer should pick his time and place.

The crying let up a little.

"What did the bastard do?"

"I'll be all right."

"I know you will because you're going to leave this place with me right now, tonight."

"Mike, you do love me?"

"I love you so much I'd cut my heart out for you."

"It's nice to have someone love you like that."

"Kitty, we've got to get away from this place."

"I know. I can't stand it any longer."

"Go put on your clothes and I'll meet you here in five minutes."

"We can't do it that way."

"Why not? You said yourself that you couldn't stand it any longer."

"If he knew I left with you he'd hunt you down and kill you. That wouldn't help us."

"Only maybe he would be the one to get killed."

"No he wouldn't. He'd hire somebody to do it. He wouldn't take any chances. He'd hire gunmen and they'd shoot you down some dark night and nobody would ever know who did it."

"But we've got to get away."

"Why don't you leave tomorrow. David said he'd give you another month's vacation before starting as his body guard."

"What about you?"

"I could meet you someplace."

"And you won't back down on me?"

"Of course not."

She looked up at me like she wanted a kiss. I held her face in my hands and kissed her, but it wasn't much of a kiss. We were so worked up that our mouths were dry.

"Where can we meet?"

"Field's would be a good place," she said.

"O.K. Meet me just inside the Randolph Street entrance at nine-thirty Monday morning."

"I'll be there."

"I'm counting on it, honey."

"Kiss me again before we go inside."

Our lips were still dry, but she knew I loved her anyway. We got up to go back inside and I thought about lying awake in my bed the rest of the night knowing that Kitty was in the next room with him. I couldn't do it.

"Kitty, I'm leaving tonight."

"Wouldn't it be better if you waited until morning?"

"I can't stand it any longer."

"I know how you must feel," she said and put her hand on my arm.

"I'll leave a note saying I decided to take the month's vacation he promised."

"I'll miss you, darling."

"Same here but it won't be for long. It's nearly morning now. We'll only be apart today and tonight and then nothing will ever separate us again."

"That's the way I want it."

I kissed her again and then went in my room to pack my clothes and write a note to David.

When I sneaked out of the house it was still dark, but you could tell from the chirping of the birds and the soft wind that it would soon be light.

As I walked down the drive to the dirt road in the rear of the house and on down the dirt road to the highway, I knew that I was still weak from my stay in the hospital. The suitcase got heavier every minute. Before I reached town I opened the bag and took out my toilet articles and a T shirt and dumped the rest by the side of the road.

When the walking was easier I felt more like thinking about Kitty and me. It was like a load had been lifted off my shoulders to know that we were going to leave David for good and make some kind of life for ourselves. It might not be the best as far as money went but it would be a good life as long as we had each other. I'd take Kitty and let the money go. A good woman was more than most men ever had.

Maybe some people would think I was a bastard for running off like that with another man's wife, but I didn't look at it that way. He should never have married her in the first place and it wasn't like they were real husband and wife. Nobody could blame a young girl like Kitty for wanting more out of life. She and I were young and full of fire and we just had to have each other.

When I finally got to the town of Lake Geneva I stopped at the station and had a cup of coffee and a sweetroll while I was waiting for the next bus for Chicago.

Because it was Sunday morning the traffic was all coming to Lake Geneva instead of leaving it, so the bus back to Chicago was nearly empty. I got a chance to catch up on some of the sleep I'd missed.

CHAPTER TEN

I GOT off the bus at the Randolph Street depot about ten o'clock Sunday morning.

I had another lonesome Sunday on my hands. There's no place in the world any deader than Chicago on a Sunday morning in the middle of the summer. And for me it was even deader than it was for the other people because I didn't know anybody in Chicago. Isn't that funny? Here I was born and brought up in the burg and I didn't know anybody. But you know how it is. The old crowd that you went to school with got all broke up during the war and somehow you just never run into them again in a city like Chicago. Maybe it's the same way in small towns too, I don't know.

Of course I did know Danny but I didn't feel quite up to seeing him. You'd think I would have been mad at him, but I wasn't. I guess he gave me what I had coming. I did run off with one of his girls.

As I walked down to Grant Park to wait for the bars to open at noon, I got to thinking about Ruth and wondering what had happened to her. I guessed she had gone back with her sister and was learning the trade. Danny was probably making love to her regularly unless he was already tired of her.

I bought some popcorn to feed the pigeons, took off my coat and sat down on a bench to watch the little bastards shimmy up to me for a free handout. I sat there looking at them wondering how they kept their feet warm in cold weather and finally got tired of the whole thing and dumped all the popcorn on the ground and let them fight over it.

I lay down on the bench and closed my eyes and I hadn't been there more than five minutes before some big flatfoot cop came over and tapped the sole of my shoe with his night stick.

"Sleeping's not allowed here," he said like he owned the town.

"Did you hear me snoring?"

"No."

"Then I wasn't asleep. I always snore when I sleep."

He pulled a pad out of his pocket.

"Bud, you wantta get run in on a vagrancy charge?"

I sat up. There wasn't any sense in getting locked up all weekend and missing Kitty on Monday.

"You'd better move on."

"I'm not sleeping. I'm Just sitting here."

"Wise guy."

"Thank you. My mother always thought I was pretty smart."

"That does it. Come on."

"I was Just leaving."

I hoisted my coat and walked away. I couldn't get in a fight with the bastard and take a chance on getting put in the tank. After I had walked almost to the street I turned around and saw him watching me. I doubled up my fist and put out one finger. He got the idea and started blowing his damn whistle. I took off across the street and then ran up Van Buren to the alley and cut back. What a hell of a town it is when a cop won't even let you sit still on a park bench.

But I knew I had asked for it. I had to find something to do or I would get myself in trouble before Monday morning. As I walked along Wabash I got to thinking about Ruth again and decided to go by the "Y" to see if I could find out anything about her.

At the "Y" I asked to see the woman in charge and the desk girl took me around back to meet a fat middle aged woman dressed in black.

"I'm looking for Miss Ruth Sims. I sent her over here about two weeks ago and now nobody knows anything about her."

"Won't you have a seat Mr...."

"Callahan's the name."

"Won't you have a seat Mr. Callahan?"

She sat down behind a desk and pulled her skirt down like she was afraid of men.

"We've been very crowded lately. Maybe I sent her someplace else. What did you say the young lady's name was?"

"Sims, Ruth Sims."

"Well, let me just have a look here."

She took some papers out of a folder on her desk and looked through them.

"You say her name was Ruth Sims?"

Christ I'd already told her a hundred times.

"That's the name."

"She was sent to a girls' club on the south side. I have a follow up note that says she was given a room there."

I got the telephone number and left.

Ruth had just gotten in from church when I called. She asked me to come out to see her.

You never saw anybody change so much in a couple of weeks. The girls there at the club ran what they called a beauty clinic and all the new members were given the once over. Ruth's long stringy hair had been cut short and it was all fluffy with little brown curls. She had touched up her eyelashes with some stuff to make her eyes look larger and the girls had made her buy a red dress with a lot of flowers on it to keep her from looking so un-filled out. The way she walked and everything was changed so she looked more like a career girl who'd been around instead of a scared little mop from down on the farm.

"You like it?" she asked.

She stood in front of me and whirled around so I could get a good look at all the changes.

"It's swell. What happened?"

"The other girls gave me some advice."

"Did they advise you about men too?"

"Yes."

"What?"

"They said a girl was smart to hold out for a ring first, but of course that was off the record."

"But it was good advice."

"You approve!"

As we left the club and walked over the soft green grass covering the center of the Midway I felt very pleased with myself because I had done one thing in my life that was unselfish and right. After all, if it hadn't been for me she would be at Danny's place taking off her clothes in front of a crowd of half drunk degenerates. I could see the change that had come over Ruth and now I was sure that she would never go back to her sister.

As we walked on over to 63rd Street to a movie she told me about the job they had helped her find at Field's.

"Of course it's not much, but I'm lucky to have it. I sell kitchen ware in the basement."

"How did they happen to give you that job?"

"I told them I was from down state Illinois and they asked me what I knew the most about. I laughed and said cooking and milking, so they put me with the kitchen ware."

"Sounds like a good idea."

"All but the money. I'd make more if I were selling women's clothes."

"One step at a time."

"That's right," she said, looking up at me and smiling. For a second I thought she pressed my hand, but I guess she didn't. That part didn't come until much later.

We saw a shoot-em-up movie and when we were outside again I said. "It sure was a shoot-em-up movie."

"It certainly was," she said and I thought about the crack Kitty had made about the movie we had seen at Lake Geneva. Kitty's remark made me feel very near to her and that she belonged to me, but Ruth's remark made me respect her a lot more. I wished to God I was more like Ruth and less like Kitty but we are what we are and I still don't know how we can do too much about it.

We stopped in one of the joints on Sixty-third Street. Ruth ordered a coke and I got a short beer. While we sat there drinking she got to talking about the things she wanted. She told me how she wanted a house and a bunch of kids someday.

"You look like you're on the way to being a career girl," I said.

"Maybe it looks that way, but you can't believe everything you see. This is just a game I'm playing till the real thing comes along."

"I hope you find the right guy."

She didn't say anything when I made that crack, but she turned her big eyes up from the table and looked at me for a long time, long enough for me to feel sort of funny inside. But Christ, she wasn't my kind of dame. It was crazy to let a good kid like Ruth make me feel funny. I'm bad medicine.

"And what do you want?"

"I want a million bucks and a blonde to spend it on.

That shut her up for a while. I ordered another beer.

"But why do you want a million dollars?"

"I just said that because it was the first thing that came to me. I don't know what in hell I want. All I know is that life's damn unsatisfactory for me like it is and a million bucks would change it. Maybe I'd be happy with a million bucks and maybe I'd be just the same."

"Do you have a girl?"

"Yeah, I got a girl."

"Tell me about her."

"She's blonde and she's beautiful and she's married to the wrong guy."

"I'm sorry for you, Mike."

"Don't waste your time, kid. I can take care of myself."

"I hope so."

"Drink up and let's go."

I don't know why it was, but suddenly she made me nervous. She was the real thing and I was such a phony.

I held her hand and we walked down the street without talking anymore. She looked in the shop windows and I just sort of followed along. After a while we cut back to the Midway and walked some more, but we didn't talk again. Talking made me think and I didn't want to think anymore right then. Kitty was going to meet me the next morning and we were going to live together forever and run a restaurant. I had the world by the tail and I didn't want to even think thoughts that might rock the boat.

After a while we ended up in front of the girl's club where Ruth lived.

"Will I see you again?" she asked when she was ready to go inside.

"What's the use?"

"I don't know."

"Look, Ruth, I'm not the kind of guy for you."

"What do you mean?"

"My psychiatrist says I'm immature."

"Your what?"

"I was just joking. I'm a sharpie and you don't want to have anything to do with guys like me whore just out for a quick buck."

"You're not that way."

"Yes I am. Good-bye."

"Let me know if you change your mind."

"Sure," I said and left.

I rode back to the Loop on the I.C. and while I was sitting there watching the back porches of the slums fly past the window I couldn't keep my mind free of thoughts. I was part bum and sharpie, but I had a little of the good in me too. Ruth made me see the good side of me, the guy that might marry a nice little girl like Ruth and settle down with a family of my own and a job where I punched the clock at eight and five. When she made me see that good side of myself it just upset me. That side of me wasn't strong enough to take over and make the rest of me behave. I didn't want to be reminded that I had more than one side. Life was hard enough without driving yourself nuts by trying to find out what you were like inside. I was a two-for-a-nickel-jerk and I'd always been a jerk and I wasn't going to get all mixed up inside thinking about houses and little white fences.

I got off the train down in the Loop and walked over to the Congress Hotel. Kitty and I might just as well have the first few days in a first class joint. Maybe it would make things easier for her.

I paid the man at the desk, bought a fifth of bonded bourbon and went the hell up to my room. I didn't get drunk that night, but I got enough of an edge on to keep from thinking anymore.

I wanted the next day to hurry and come so I could have Kitty again. I was awful lonesome that night.

CHAPTER ELEVEN

THAT lousy feeling left me the next morning when I met Kitty at Field's. I had stood there at the Randolph Street entrance for half an hour waiting for her and I had about decided that she had changed her mind when suddenly she walked through the revolving door and smiled at me. She looked good that day, like a shiny new penny that had never left the mint. She was dressed up in a pale blue silk dress and wore white earrings and a string of white shell beads. For a minute she just stood there and looked at me and then she ran to me and threw her arms around my neck and held me like she had found the thing that she had always wanted. We were so much in love that we walked down Michigan Boulevard with ours arms still around each other. It even made the people happy who saw us. They would look our way and then smile like they were remembering a time when they had been in love like us. Only nobody was ever as in love as Kitty and I were that day. There could have been another Chicago fire and an earthquake thrown in on top of it and it wouldn't have pulled us away from each other's arms.

When we got to my room at the Congress Hotel she could hardly wait. First thing when we went in the room she put her arms around my neck again and pushed her hips up against me and moved them back and forth a little till I damn near blew a gasket.

"It's our day," I said.

"It'll always be our day."

"Let's never miss a day making love."

"Never, and let's not miss any afternoons either."

"Honey, take it off. Take it off quick."

This time I didn't have to beg her. She stood right there in the middle of the room and undressed and by the time she was naked I was too. Like a couple of kinds we ran and jumped on the bed.

"I want a drink," she said after I kissed her. I didn't want a drink right then, but she was mine and I could wait a couple of minutes.

My hand was shaking when I opened the dresser drawer and took out the bourbon. I poured us about four fingers each, went in the bathroom for some ice water and came back to the bed.

"To us," she said and held out her glass.

"To the two people who own the whole damned world."

"And to all the beds we'll make love in."

"Forever and ever."

We each took a long drink. This time when I kissed her, her mouth was cold from the drink, but it didn't stay that way long.

"I want so much to please you," she muttered as I kissed her neck and then let my kisses go on southward. "Darling, you're going to make me die."

"I'm going to make you die a million deaths."

"And I'll love everyone of them."

She shivered and squirmed back and forth from her fluttering eyelids all the way down to her upturned toes.

I poured the bourbon over her chest and she screamed with pleasure as I lapped it off her skin, attacking the little pools of bourbon last.

"Mike, every time we make love I want it to be different."

"You're my woman."

"What can I do to please you? Just tell me all the things I can do to please you. I don't know and you'll have to tell me."

"This," I said.

She had never even heard of such pleasures but it was wonderful. She was completely free and everything was wonderful. She was soaring in the sky and I was right there with her.

"Mike, you're killing me," she said and arched up in the bed, unable to stand the torture of the pleasure which fired through her body.

"Now, now, now …."

And she was like a machine gun ….

When I woke up I felt the best I'd ever felt. It was like I had taken a bath with Lifebuoy in a fresh mountain stream. I had everything. I was the richest man in the world. I was the youngest, the strongest, the purest. I was God Almighty. If I could keep Kitty with me all my life that was all I cared about. The rest of the guys could have their listings in Who's Who and their million bucks as long as I had Kitty. I didn't want to ever look at another woman or take another drink. I didn't need it. I was complete.

That was the way things went all week.

"If we don't start looking for a hash house pretty soon there won't be any money left," I said one night when we came in from blowing forty bucks at the Club Carnival.

"We can use the money I have in the bank."

"How much is that?"

"I don't know."

"How much would you guess?"

"Darling, I don't know much about things like money. I never think about it."

"Like hell you don't."

"All right then I do, but let's not talk about it now."

She took off her clothes and stood there in front of me making pixie eyes at me. She was the cutest little she-devil in the whole wide world and she was all mine.

"Do you care about things like money?" she asked, coming up close to me and undoing my tie.

"We've got to live."

"Aren't you living?"

Oh, yes, I was living all right. I threw her across the bed without bothering to take off my clothes and we both lived a little. Half an hour later we lived a little more. We were living so damned much I was soon going to be dead if we kept it up like this.

"Turn over," I said.

At breakfast the next morning I bought a paper and settled down to look for a place to buy. Honeymoons were O.K., but a guy couldn't stay on one forever. It was like eating chocolate sundaes three times a day.

"There's a restaurant for sale over on Wilson Avenue."

She didn't say anything. I looked up at her. She was toying with her grapefruit and had a far away look in her eyes.

"Did you hear me?"

"What was that?"

"I said there's a restaurant for sale over on Wilson Avenue."

"So?"

"Well aren't you interested at all?"

"What do you want me to do, turn hand springs?"

"No, but I expect you to take a little interest."

"All right."

"This place on Wilson can be bought for a grand."

"It sounds like what we want."

"Would you mind being that close to Memorial Hospital?"

"Why not?"

"I thought you might feel funny slinging hash for your old pals."

"They eat at the hospital, but where do you get this slinging hash business? You think I'm going to be a waitress?"

"You are until we can afford to hire one."

She didn't say anything, but I could tell hash slinging wasn't what she expected at the end of the rainbow. Here she'd married a guy worth a million bucks and now she was down to slinging hash to live with the man she loved. Not many dames love a guy enough to give up a million. I decided I must be a pretty good man where it counted.

"All right, let's get started," she said and got up to dress.

Before we went to the place that was for sale we stopped by the bank to see how much she had in her savings account. It came to $34.05 and the man said she wouldn't be able to get it without her pass book. A hell of a fine note that was. Here I'd been spending my reward money like water with the idea that she had a few hundred tucked away. I checked my wallet and found we had a little over seven hundred left. But that was all right. Nobody ever expected to sell a place for what they asked.

We caught a Ravenswood bus on Michigan Boulevard and got off at the end of the line. This hash joint I read about was across the street from the Marshall Field Clinic. It was a good neighborhood, but this particular hash joint wasn't much. There was a big sign outside that advertised Coca Cola and in smell letters underneath it said: Joe Papanicholo's. Down on the glass by the door there was another sign that said: Ladies Invited. So you know the kind of joint it was.

The place was closed. But by the time the door was loose from my knocking, a dumpy little Greek woman with white hair came out from back of the partition in the rear and asked us what we wanted.

"I see in the paper this place is up for sale."

"That's right," she said in a foreign accent and was suddenly all smiles like a sharpie that's found a sucker. "Come right on in."

You should have seen the inside. There was dust all over everything. Nothing had been touched for about a hundred years.

"Looks a little deserted," I said. Kitty looked around like the place made her sick inside.

"My husband he's been sick," the old woman said. "It's a little dirty but everything's she is in fine shape underneath."

"Yeah, I'll bet it is."

"You want to talk to Joe? That's my husband."

Kitty and I followed the white haired woman to the back where she opened a door and motioned for us to go on in.

A skinny old man lay propped up in a tiny bed with sheets so dirty that they looked like last year's snow. He couldn't move the left side of his body and when he spoke, he drooled out of the corner of his mouth. The woman introduced us but she did all the talking.

"You see you folks can five back here and save money that way. We throw the furniture in the bargain. Eh, Joe?"

"Thatsa right," he said and smiled at us out of the good side of his face.

"You get everything you need for thousand dollar," the wife continued. "Soundsa good, no?"

"We'll think it over," I said. "We have a couple of other places to look at before we make up our minds."

Kitty still had a sour look on her face when we left the joint and took a Damen Avenue bus down to the Polish district around Halsted and Division to look at another place. She didn't say anything about the restaurant and when I asked her what was wrong she wouldn't answer me. Some women are that way. They're all smiles and laughs when it comes to pretty clothes and a night club but when they see life like it is, they want to close their pretty little eyes and think about something nicer.

The place we looked at on Halsted Street was in about the same class as the one on Wilson, only the neighborhood wasn't nearly as good. But what kind of fixtures could I expect for seven hundred G's? But I didn't plan to spend the rest of my lousy life in one of those fire traps. I just wanted something to get started with. I'd work up from those dumps to the big time.

When we ate lunch and went back to the hotel I tried to explain to Kitty that a guy couldn't start at the top unless he was born with a bankroll. She didn't say anything.

"Well say something."

She just stayed clammed up.

"God-damn it, if you're going in this with me I want to know what you think about it."

She still wouldn't say anything. I went over to where she was sitting by the window and shook her hard. It didn't do any good. She started crying and I felt like hell.

"Honey, I want you to be happy. Please tell me what you think about the places. Do you want to take one of them or keep on looking?"

"Mike, I can't do it," she sobbed.

"What do you mean?"

"I can't live in one of those filthy holes and wait on tables and cook."

"We can clean up either one of the places. You know, put up some bright red curtains and things and make them look nice."

She really started crying when I said that.

"What's the matter, honey?"

She went over to the dresser and got a handkerchief from her pocketbook. After she wiped her eyes I asked her again what the trouble was.

"It's just that you're such a nice guy, Mike."

"Nice guy hell. I'm just another jerk, but it happens that I love you."

"Mike, I can't do it."

"O.K., we'll look for another place."

"I mean I can't five in any kind of place we can buy for the amount of money we have."

"Let's look again tomorrow before you make up your mind."

"I couldn't stand it even if we saw a place that was twice as good as the ones we found today."

I reached in my pocket for a butt, thumped it on the back of my hand and lighted it. I took a long drag. I guess I was stalling for time, because I didn't want to hear the part that I knew was coming next.

"You mean we're all washed up?" I asked.

"Mike, I don't ever want to leave you."

"O.K., tell me your plan."

"Let's go back home. You take the job as body guard and we'll keep on seeing each other."

"We tried that once, and it didn't work."

"But this time it will work. I love you too much to ever live without you again."

"It won't be so easy to go back this time."

"Why?"

"Didn't you tell David that you were running away?"

"No. I told him I was going to see my mother in St. Louis."

"So you never planned to really run away with me after all."

"I wanted to give us a few days to look for a place. I knew that things might not turn out and I didn't want to tell David till I was sure."

I didn't like that. It was one thing for her to leave David and run away with me, but it was something else to be dishonest about it. I may be a jerk and a cheat, but at least I don't try to fool myself about it. When I look in the mirror every morning I don't try to turn the face I see into a priest's. I don't like the way she was dishonest with herself and David, but I didn't say anything about it. I should have known enough to pull out and leave her right then.

I did think of calling it quits, of telling her to make up her mind about what she wanted and take the consequences. But she was so damn beautiful and young and innocent that I knew she must be pure and lovely inside. I thought that she was just a poor kid caught in a cross fire that she couldn't handle.

"What if you can't stand living with both of us?"

"I'll be able to handle it this time."

"What if you can't? Suppose you have to decide between me and David?"

"Don't you know the answer?"

"I thought I did."

"I'll take you every time. And just think what we'll have someday. David is a sick man with his diabetes and he can't live very much longer. When he dies we'll be richer than you ever dreamed of. Well have ten or maybe fifteen million dollars. Just imagine it, ten million dollars at the very least. Think how we'll be able to live then—Monte Carlo, Paris, Rome, Switzerland. Oh God, Mike, can you blame me for wanting to wait for that?"

"I guess not, kid."

But I knew something would go wrong. You just don't get ten million bucks that easy.

CHAPTER TWELVE

T HAT NIGHT we didn't make love. Somehow it just wasn't the same. The next morning Kitty went back to her place on Sheridan Road. I bummed around town for a couple of days and then went back to David and told him I had had enough vacation and was ready to go to work as his body guard. That put me in a different class from a chauffeur, because I would have to be seen in public with him and he wanted me to look like a companion instead of a body guard.

The first thing he did was to send me to see a gun smith who had a shop over on West Van Buren. This guy had some of the loveliest heaters I ever set eyes on. I looked them all over, the Colts, the Smith and Westerns, all of them. When I picked up a blue forty-five revolver I knew I had the right one.

"That's enough to hunt elephants with," the little grey-haired man said when I told him I liked the forty-five. "Why if you just hit a man in the little finger with a bullet from that gun it would be enough to knock him down."

I gripped the gun and aimed it. The balance was perfect.

"Got used to this kind when I was in the army."

"You ever shoot anybody with one of them?"

"I killed a German in the Hertgan Forest with a gun like this. I got cut off from my unit one day and walked into a platoon of Krauts. While I was trying to get away from them and find my outfit I lost my carbine, but I still had a forty-five like this in my belt. I ran up a gully and when I came to the end of it there was this damn Kraut standing right in front of me. We saw each other at about the same time. I pulled my forty-five out and almost shot him in two."

I held the gun up and pulled the trigger like I was shooting the guy again. The hammer fell with a loud click.

"I hate to think what a gun like that could do to a man's stomach," the little guy said.

"O.K. if I take this one?"

"Mr. Grey's secretary said to give you anything you wanted."

"Good. I'll take the forty-five."

"You'll need a case. Shoulder or belt?"

"I got used to a belt holder. Any here for me to look at?"

I showed him the gun license David had given me and left the shop with the gun on my side. It was so big you could see it bulge way the hell out underneath my coat.

My next stop was at a tailor's joint on the third floor of a building down on State Street.

He was about thirty-five, tall and skinny with long fingers and hair that would have made Tarzan proud to own. He had to get on his knees to measure my waist and every time his head came near the forty- five I had belted on my waist he would wrinkle up his nose and pull away a little like he was scared. That gun made me feel like a big son of a bitch.

After leaving there I loaded the gun. I walked a little straighter than usual. There wasn't anything in the world I was afraid of. I wished Danny would sick some more of his goons on me. I had a license to carry a gun and they didn't. Even the law was on my side.

Things changed after I got my new standing. Karl was nicer to me. But I didn't see much of Kitty. That is I didn't see much of her for the first few days.

Then one night about one o'clock the telephone in my room over the garage rang. I pulled myself up and sat on the side of the bed a minute to wake up. I shook my head and staggered over to where the phone sat ringing its head off.

"Yeah?"

"Mike come over right away," Kitty's voice said.

"What's the matter?" Suddenly I was wide awake.

"Just come over right away," she said and banged the receiver down so hard it nearly blew out my ear drum.

I threw on some clothes, ran down the steps three at a time and raced over the lawn to the back door.

Karl was standing there to let me in. He was tall and haughty. He wore a maroon dressing gown and did not seem the least bit upset.

"What's going on?" I asked him.

He looked at me and a thin smile crossed his dark face.

"Mr. Grey is about to die."

"Christ," I said and pushed past him into the house.

I found Kitty walking back and forth in David's room. He lay on his back on the bed. His mouth was open. He was breathing fast and his skin had a lead color to it.

"Is he unconscious?" I asked and ran over to the bed to feel his pulse like feeling his pulse would tell me what to do for him.

"Yes."

"What happened?"

"He's in a diabetic coma."

"Did you call the doctor?"

"Yes. He said to take him to the hospital right away."

"Tell Karl to come up and help me. He's too fat for me to carry downstairs alone."

Kitty just kept walking back and forth like she didn't know where she was. I went out into the hall and shouted down for Karl to come help me.

"I'll be there as soon as I put my shirt on," he called back.

"Well hurry the hell up."

In a couple of minutes he came upstairs. I took David's chest and Karl carried his legs. We managed to get him downstairs, but it wasn't easy because he was so fat and limp. We shoved him in the back seat of the car. I drove. We went down Sheridan Road like a hurricane. When we got to Foster I just held the horn down and kept my foot on the gas.

It wasn't till we got him in the emergency room at the hospital that I laughed at myself and wondered why I was in such a hurry to save his life. I guess it's just a reflex to help people. But my own life would have been a lot simpler if he had died then.

We put David on a stretcher and the orderly rolled him upstairs. Kitty and Karl and I sat around the room while Dr. Saunders examined the patient and ordered some lab work.

They kept giving him more insulin and intravenous fluids. By four o'clock he was conscious again. His skin was no longer grey and the breathing was normal, but his face had an ungodly puffiness about it that made you feel like he was a man come back to earth from the next world.

"The doctor says he's going to be all right," Kitty said after talking with Dr. Saunders out in the hall.

"Should I stay here to watch him?"

"Nobody's going to bother him here in the hospital."

Karl kept looking at us like he was storing up every move we made so he could tell it to David later.

"He pays me to watch him."

"Don't worry," she said.

"Do you want me to drive you home?"

"I'm worn out. Let's go. We won't be able to do anymore for him now."

Kitty and Karl sat in the back seat of the caddy while I drove. I didn't mind chauffeuring for Kitty, but it graveled me to have Karl sit back there chatting with Kitty like he owned the string of hotels. It reminded me of the time David was in Hot Springs when I walked in the living room and found Karl sitting in the big chair smoking a cigar. If David ever did die and I married Kitty, I would sure kick Karl to kingdom come.

Kitty and I were real strict around Karl. When I drove up to the mansion, I got out and opened the door. As Karl stepped out he smiled and I was sure he liked it. He and Kitty went in the house. I put the car away and went up to my room over the garage.

I poured a drink, took off my tie and sat there on the bed for a long time thinking of what would have happened to me if David had died. I would have waited for a few months and then married Kitty. I tried to picture ten million bucks. I took a buck out of my wallet and measured it and then multiplied it by ten million and then figured out how many times they would go around the earth if they were put end to end. Ten million bucks is a lot of green stuff. I remembered my old lady when I was a kid. Saturday night was her big night in the tavern. If she didn't make it that night, she didn't make it all week. I remembered when she would count up the dough. If it came to thirty-five, she broke even. If she hit fifty, it was big stuff. But if it was twenty-five, it meant that we ate beans and potatoes all week. Yes, ten million bucks was a lot of money.

I fit a cigarette and looked out over the lake towards the east where a thin grey line was starting the day. There was a soft off-shore breeze and you could hear the birds waking up. I heard a noise behind me and jerked around.

Kitty was standing there in the door. After closing it, she leaned against the door and took a long drag off of the cigarette she held.

"Expecting a cold spell?" I asked.

"You mean the coat I'm wearing?"

"Yes."

She opened it. The coat and the high heeled shoes were all she was wearing. She put a hand on each hip, spread her legs a little and just stood there looking at me. She was a real blonde all right.

When I got up from the bed and went over to her, she pulled the coat together again and folded her arms.

"I can't do anything but look?"

"I need a drink, Mike."

"You're sure you want to D.F.?"

"Yes. Don't kiss me yet," she said and pulled away from me. She sat down cross-legged on the bed while I threw a couple of drinks together.

We drank about half of it and all the time she kept looking at me in a funny way.

"Mike, how much do you love me?" she asked after a while.

"Don't you know?"

"Tell me."

"I love you with everything there is and you know it. I'd cut it off up to here for you."

"Would you love me no matter what I have done?"

"I love you, period. No *if, ands* or *buts* about it."

"Would you do anything I asked?"

"Why the hose treatment? You know I love you."

She took another cigarette and lighted it off of the butt of the one she was smoking. Then she sipped the whiskey.

"Mike, I tried to kill David," she said and took a long drag off the cigarette. She squinted her eyes a little and watched me close as she let the blue smoke come lazily out of her mouth.

The words hit me like an earthquake. Suddenly when the word KILL is spoken every damn thing is changed. I could feel it change in me. I could feel an icicle start at the base of my brain and work its way down my spinal column and then separate and go down each of my legs.

I didn't say anything. I got up and began walking back and forth like I was trying to get away from the whirling pool inside me. I wanted to open the door and go outside in the cool morning air and then wash all the blackness out of my mind by taking a dip in the lake. Somehow I had felt all along that we would end up by killing David, but now that the time had come to put it into words, I wanted to leave.

I forced myself to sit down on the bed beside Kitty.

"Do you want to hear about it?" she asked.

No, I didn't want to hear about it. I wanted to dump her and leave and then I asked myself what kind of a yellow hearted jerk I was. This wasn't me turning yellow. I was supposed to be tough. I could take it and I could dish it out. It was like pulling myself down by the collar and telling myself to sit still and listen.

"Yeah, I want to hear about it," I said in a hoarse voice. I lighted a cigarette and looked away from her as she talked.

'I diluted his insulin. I poured three fourths of it out and then filled the bottle up with water."

"So he wasn't getting near enough of the stuff?"

"That's right. In two days he went in a coma. It would have worked. He would have been dead by morning if Karl hadn't discovered him."

"Does Karl suspect anything?"

"No."

"You're certain?"

"How could he?"

"I don't know. I was just checking."

"It's the smoothest plan in the world to kill a diabetic."

"I guess so."

She must have seen the dead look on my face. I still couldn't look at her. After a minute she reached over and turned my face around to her.

"Do you still love me?" she asked.

Sure.

"Sure, but what?" she asked.

"Well, what the hell! I'm new at this killing game. You can't expect me to act like you just told me you had a cup of Lipton's tea after supper."

"But you do still love me?"

"Yes."

"I was doing it for us. If he had died we could have been married and we would have been rich. Not wealthy, rich."

I kept puffing on the fag and didn't answer her.

"Mike, I tried to make a go of it without killing him. It just wouldn't work out for us as long as he was alive. You know I did it for us."

"Yeah, I know." I wished to hell I had stayed in L. A. and hooked in with the syndicate like a bright boy. With those boys you got professional killers to do your dirty work. I knew what was coming next.

"Mike, he was sick. He won't live much longer anyway. Killing him wouldn't be cruel like it would be to kill a well man."

"What's next?" I asked.

"Mike, you've got to kill him."

Like I said before, I knew what she was going to say next, but still the words were hail stones.

As I poured another drink I had to concentrate hard to keep my hand from shaking. I downed half a glass of the hot stuff.

"Fix me one too," she said.

I mixed two more. I handed her one drink and walked up and down the floor drinking mine.

"Mike, you need guts to get anywhere in this world. It's not easy. If you can't take what you want, you won't ever have anything." She paused for a minute. "Remember that first day I met you?"

"Yeah." Yeah I remembered it. It was about a thousand years ago.

"That very first day I knew you were a man with guts."

"I am. I'll do it," I said. Christ what else could I say? I was already in it up to here. I was so crazy in love with Kitty that I would do anything. I was so much in love that I would kill a man to take away his wife. It was the world's oldest solution to the world's oldest problem.

"I knew you were man enough to do it. A woman really knows a man loves her when he'll kill for her."

"O.K., I'll kill him. Now let's not talk about it anymore."

"All right, Mike. Come over here and sit down beside me."

She had that same mean look to her face that she had the first afternoon I had met her. At that time I had thought she was mean. Later I thought she was just a lonesome kid. Now I knew she was a little of both.

When I walked over to the bed I had that same feeling of wanting to hit her that I had had that first afternoon. We finished off a couple more drinks. We hadn't had anything to eat in a hell of a long time and the drinks really told. But they didn't take away that desire I had to hit her.

I couldn't stand it any longer. I got up from where my head lay in her lap. I kneeled on the bed and looked down at her for a long second and then I struck her on the side of the face with my open hand. It felt so good that I hit her again as she was going down.

"God, I love you," she said.

When I kissed her I could taste the sweet blood that covered her lips.

"You bitch," I said and kissed her again.

"Oh God, I love you, Mike."

"I love you like sin and I hate you like hell," I said and slapped her again. She was the beginning and the end: with her I had first lived and with her I was going to die. I could feel it come through the room like a blast of cold air chilling my neck.

"Hit me again Mike."

This time I didn't hold back. I really let her have one. She smiled up at me.

"My man."

I punched her in the stomach and then threw myself down beside her and began kissing her like crazy.

"Mike, make love to me."

I made love to her alright; angry love, love that was half hate and half love, the kind of love that includes everything.

"Mike, make me scream."

What I did next made her scream alright, and it hurt more than she thought it would and she really meant it when she screamed, but she loved it.

CHAPTER THIRTEEN

KITTY and I planned to kill David. I knew that it still wasn't too late for me to pull up stakes and haul my rear out of there, but I didn't do it. I wanted Kitty and I wanted ten million bucks. Strange as it sounds though, I wanted something else more. I wanted to prove to myself that I was man enough to want something and get it.

David looked like hell when he came home from the hospital. He still had the same pudgy face, but it wasn't rosy any longer. It was pale and white and his hair was completely grey like the thin grey hair of an old man. His leg was worse. Now he walked with a crutch and limped more than he had before. Sometimes I felt like Kitty was right when she said we were doing him a favor to kill him. He should be put away.

Thursday was the new chauffeur's day off. When he was away I drove David. One Thursday afternoon I was taking an after dinner snooze in my room when the phone rang.

"The chief wants you to drive him to the Loop," Karl said.

"O.K., I'll be there in a minute."

"Make it snappy," Karl said so he would get in the last word.

I backed the Caddy out of the garage and parked it in the drive beside the house while I went up to the door to help David down to the car. By the time I got him out on the porch, Kitty had come out to help me. You should have seen the way she looked when she had on her town clothes. She was wearing a green linen dress and had on a red straw hat as big as an umbrella and she looked as fresh and virginal as a snow covered Christmas morning. She took one of his arms and we helped the old man down the stairs. She sort of glanced at me while he was stepping into the car. I wondered what she had planned. I had the method for killing him all worked out in my own mind, but I wanted to see if she had a better plan.

"David, I want Mike to drive me over to Teller's," she said when we stopped in front of the building where David's office was located.

"Hadn't I better stick with Mr. Grey," I said to make it sound O.K.

"Surely I'll be safe in my own office," he said and laughed with a pained expression on his face like it hurt him to laugh.

"Anything you say, sir."

"You drive Mrs. Grey wherever she wants to go. I'll be all right."

The doorman opened the car door.

"Do you want me to help you inside?"

"Paul will be enough. You two act like I've got one foot in the grave," he said and laughed again as the doorman took his arm.

After David got out of the car I drove on down the block towards the lake and then turned north on the Outer Drive.

"You really want to go to Teller's?"

"Let's go someplace where we can talk."

"We can park near the beach on North Avenue."

"That's all right with me."

The rain was coming down in a fine drizzle. The wind was from the northeast and was dashing high waves against the breakwater along the Outer Drive. We were the only ones in sight when I drew up in the parking lot at the North Avenue Beach.

I turned around to look at her.

"What's your plan?" I asked.

"Come on back here with me."

"It would be a pleasure."

I opened the door and crawled in back with her. She looked up at me like she wanted it right there, but we didn't have time. We had to talk turkey and talk it fast.

"O.K., let's stick to business," I said.

"What do you have in mind?"

"I thought we should plan it so the police would think he was killed by the syndicate. It's a good set up for that. He kicked them out of one of his hotels because they were found running bookie service in one of the suites. After that he hired me as a body guard because he was afraid of them."

"It sounds like a good idea," she said.

"To make it look like a syndicate killing I'd have to shoot him down on the street someplace."

"How could you do that if you were supposed to be his body guard?"

"Easy. I could stop the car in front of a drug store and go in for some cigarettes. I could say that he was knocked off while I was in the store."

"They would check on that. The man who sold you the cigarettes would say he didn't hear the blast while you were in the store."

"That's right. I hadn't thought of an angle like that."

"You could pretend to find something wrong with the car and get out to check on it."

"That's an idea," I said. The whole thing was beginning to take shape now that I was talking about it. I pulled out a pack of butts, gave one to Kitty and we both leaned back in the seat trying to think the thing through.

"I'd have to use a shot gun. What would I do with it after the killing?"

"You might strap it under the car."

"Too risky. They might search the car."

"I could give it to you. That would be the best plan. You park across the street from where I stop. After I shoot him, I'll give you the gun and you can drive away. It would look better for someone to see a get away car leaving."

"Would it be safe?"

"Sure. You'd have a good head start on anybody that would follow. Besides who would follow a get away car other than the police?"

"That's right. We could kill him near the house so I could drive straight home and put the car in the garage."

"This is beginning to sound good."

And it did sound good. The kind of murders that were done on the street with a shotgun blast were hardly ever solved. No clues would be left. Even the cops wouldn't expect to get an arrest. There would be the usual rounding up of hoods for questioning. The papers would play it up for a few days and gradually the whole thing would blow over.

We talked on for a few minutes about our plans. It was taking shape now and I knew I would be able to do it. I felt like we were talking about a movie or something that didn't really have anything to do with me. Pretty soon I looked at my watch and said that it was time for us to go back to pick up David.

Kitty wanted to right then while we were in the back seat of the car. She was always ready and she always appreciated it.

"We'd better get back," I said.

Then I looked over and saw that she had her skirt pulled up around her waist. There wasn't anything under it but a garter belt and what you would expect. Damn it, I wanted to turn her down but I just couldn't do it once she started acting this way.

I looked around and didn't see anybody. By this time she had done things to my trousers and was sitting on my lap facing me. I watched while she ground her teeth together, threw her head to one side, squeezed her eyes tight together and in general looked like a woman dying of pain instead of pleasure.

This was certainly no place for it. We were the only car on the parking lot and stood out like a mountain in Kansas. When you've been talking about killing someone it doesn't leave you exactly relaxed.

While we were making love I kept glancing out the windows and finally saw a prowl car turn in from the Outer Drive.

"Baby, here come the cops," I said. The words didn't seem to make any difference. I tried to pull away from her but she dug her nails in my back and squeezed me to her with all her animal strength.

"Kitty, the cops are coming!"

And then she gave out with that deep moan of hers and relaxed her grip on me. Quickly I slid out from under her and fixed myself. Just as I finished with my zipper the prowl car parked beside us and a cop came jumping out like he had discovered gold. We looked decent, but our faces were still excited enough to give us away.

I rolled down the window.

"What's going on in there?" the angular faced cop asked, looking down at me.

I wanted to blow his head off. What right did he have to go around poking his head in places that were none of his business? He knew damn well what had been going on and now he wanted to come over to enjoy the scene. I guess he got his pleasure out of keeping other people from having any.

I wanted to kill him so bad I couldn't even talk.

"Why nothing, officer," Kitty said and smiled up at him.

"You married to this man?" The cop pointed to me with his night stick.

"Certainly."

"Then why don't you take him home if you want to kiss him?"

"I'm just very sentimental about this spot. You see, we used to come here while we were courting."

"Let's see your driver's license," he said to me.

I showed it to him.

"Chauffeur, eh?"

"That's right."

"This your car?"

"It's the boss' car."

He stood around for five minutes annoying us like that, waiting for Kitty to beg him.

"I really ought to run you two in. There's something funny going on here."

"Please, officer," she said and looked up at him with her blue eyes. "We weren't doing anything. Be a good sport and forget about it."

He thought for a minute and looked Kitty up and down like he was trying to make up his mind about something.

"What's going on, Mac?" the other cop said, strolling up to the window.

"Nothing. It's O.K.," the first cop said.

"You two move on and don't let me catch you down here again," the cop said to us.

"Thank you officer," Kitty said.

They walked back to the patrol car as I climbed out and got in the front seat.

"The damn bastards," I said.

"It's all right," Kitty said and looked back to see if they had gone.

I drove fast going back down to the hotel and then I gradually got over my anger and forgot about the incident until later.

That night in my room I thought about our plan a lot. I couldn't see any loop holes. I'd blow his head off some rainy afternoon and that would be the end of the whole thing. Kitty and I would wait a reasonable time before we got married. Then we would take a trip to Europe or somewhere so we could forget about David and everything that was his. Kitty and I would have a good life together. There wouldn't be any more loneliness for me. I would have her in bed every night. We would make love and then go to sleep there in each other's arms. Now at last my life was beginning to get some place.

And David—well he was so sick we would be doing him a favor to put him out of his misery.

I opened a new bottle of cheap bar whiskey and as I sat down by the window to drink the highball I thought about the kind of bourbon I would be drinking the rest of my life. Everything was going to be different. Yes, every damn thing was going to change.

I thought about the gun I would use to kill David. It would have to be a shotgun because that was what the syndicate always used. And besides, it was very efficient. I'd have to buy one; that wouldn't be a very good idea because I planned to kill him right away. I thought of going down on the south side and getting one at a sporting goods shop, but then I changed my mind. I would have to go someplace where the Chicago papers weren't read. My picture might possibly get in the paper some way. The news hounds always played up a juicy killing for all it was worth. They might show a picture of the man who was with him at the time of the killing and I wouldn't want some guy to see me in the paper and then call the police station and tell them that he had sold me a gun the week before the killing. That just wouldn't look good.

Then I got another idea. If I used somebody else's gun nobody would know anything about it.

The next day I got David to call a friend of his on the park commission. He saw to it that I got a membership in the skeet club that overlooks the lake from the Outer Drive. I went down a couple of times and shot a few targets. It was good to get a gun in my hands again. After ten minutes I had the swing of the thing and was able to hit targets five out of six tries.

The instructor loaned me a Remington repeater that seemed to fit my hands. After practicing with it for two afternoons I was ready for something that walked.

Wednesday night I cleaned the gun, loaded it with seven, twelve gauge shells, put the safety catch on and stashed the gun away in the trunk of the Caddy.

The next day was Thursday. The chauffeur would be off and it would be up to me to drive David down to the Loop and back. It would be his last trip.

That night I finished half a bottle of rot gut so I could sleep.

CHAPTER FOURTEEN

KITTY and I had it all planned out. When I drove him back from the office I would tell him his wife wanted me to stop on the way home for a package of cigarettes. That would give me an excuse to go over to Broadway instead of on out Sheridan Road like we usually traveled. I would stop for the cigarettes and then cut down Catalpa, a side street that leads to Sheridan Road. I was to say something was wrong with the motor and stop the car on Catalpa. Kitty was to be parked across the street. I would take the gun out of the trunk, shoot David and give her the gun. She was to go up Kenmore in her car, cut over to Sheridan at the next block and then go the three blocks to home where she would put the car in the garage and leave the gun off in my room.

It was a perfect plan because it was the way the professionals did it.

It was a beautiful day for murder. The sky turned a Mediterranean blue and the air was cleaned by a breeze that was fresh from a three hundred mile sweep down the lake. It was such a nice day that David decided to sit out on the back lawn that overlooked the lake rather than go down to the Loop.

At ten o'clock I went out to the back yard to find out if he was going to sit there all day.

"How is the skeet shooting?" he asked me when he looked up and saw me.

"Fine, sir."

"Great sport skeet shooting. I used to do some myself."

"Would you like to go down to the club with me for a try at it sometime?"

"Too old for that sort of thing any longer. Shooting's for you young bucks."

He took a cigarette from the jacket he was wearing. I lighted it for him.

"Did I ever tell you about my safari?"

"I don't believe you did, sir."

"Spent six weeks in Africa one time. Beautiful place Africa. Wonderful shooting in those days. The best part was shooting a rhinoceros. Let the fellow charge right at me. Makes you feel you're being charged by a freight train. Shot him down in his tracks with a .505. Ever shoot a .505?"

"No, sir. I never have."

"The kick almost knocks you down."

"I'll bet it does."

He went on to tell me about all the gazelles and antelopes that he shot. While he was telling me about the lion he got, Karl brought a pot of coffee and a cup out.

"Have some coffee, Mike?" he asked me when he had pulled his chair up to the table that sat there on the lawn.

"Thank you, sir. That would be swell."

Karl gave me one of his blackest looks. Without saying anything he went back in the house and returned with a cup for me.

"Thanks, Karl," I said.

"Maybe you would like some cream and sugar," David said. "Of course the doctor won't let me have anything but saccharine."

"I could use some cream and sugar," I said. "I'll go in and get it."

"Nothing of the sort. Karl will bring you some. Won't you Karl?"

"Yes, sir," he said and turned stiffly to go back to the house.

I enjoyed the coffee very much. It seemed a shame that I was going to have to kill David instead of Karl.

We talked on about shooting while we finished the coffee.

"Plan to go down to the Loop today?" I asked after lighting a cigarette.

"Almost too pretty to spend any time in the office today."

"That's right. Beautiful day."

I got away from him as soon as I could. If we couldn't get him downtown we would have to wait until the next Thursday to kill him. I couldn't stand the suspense that long.

I found Kitty upstairs in her studio where she was painting china dolls.

"You shouldn't come up here," she said.

"David's not going downtown today."

"Then we'll just have to wait until next week."

"If were going to do it, we've got to do it today."

"Getting yellow?"

"Hell no. I just want to finish with it."

"If we have to wait, we just have to wait."

"Can you get out of the house for a few minutes?"

"I guess so."

"Go to the drug store and call the house. Tell whoever answers that you are calling from the office and that you need Mr. Grey to sign some papers. That way he'll have to go downtown."

"They'll recognize my voice."

"Put a pack of gum in your mouth. That will disguise your voice."

She thought for a minute.

"At the inquest someone might mention that he got a phony call."

"So what? The police will think it's somebody from the syndicate."

"All right. I'll leave in a few minutes."

I went back to my room and started walking the floor like a caged lion. I smoked about a hundred fags and finally broke down and took a drink. While I was screwing the top back on I looked out the window and saw Karl come up to David and say something. David then braced himself against his crutch and pulled his fat body out of the chair and started walking slowly towards the house.

I smoked another cigarette and took another swig before my phone rang.

"Yes?"

"Mr. Grey would like to go downtown," Karl's voice said.

"O.K." I was about to hang up. "By the way, Karl, I enjoyed the coffee."

"I'll get you," he said in a muffled voice and hung up.

Like hell he would get me. He didn't know that I would be the boss in a couple more hours.

As I drove David downtown he was in a very good humor. He joked with me and asked me questions.

"You never say anything about your girl," he said as we turned right on Foster to go on to the Outer Drive. "You do have a girl?"

"Yes, sir."

"Tell me about her. Are you going to get married one of these days?"

"I'm thinking about it," I said. I didn't say that I was planning to marry his wife in a couple of months.

"What's she like?"

"Blonde, blue eyes, cute."

"Sounds attractive. Sometimes I wish I were a young man again."

"You must not be too old if you married a girl Mrs. Grey's age."

"Just memories, that's all I have anymore."

He lighted a cigar and then leaned back in the seat again with a sigh.

"This is just between you and me," he said.

"Yes, sir."

"If a man can't have a few secrets with his body guard, I don't know who he can have secrets with."

"That's right."

"Kitty was quite a girl when I first married her. She's meant a lot to me as time has gone by. Of course she doesn't mean the same to me now that she once did."

"I don't understand you."

"Well, you know, I'm getting old." He paused for a minute. "Sometimes I think it wasn't fair for me to get her tied down with an old man like me."

"She seems happy most of the time."

"I guess so. But she's just a child. It doesn't take much to make her happy."

No it didn't take much—only a man my age and ten million bucks!

"Sometimes I feel as though I do not understand her very well," he continued. "There's such a difference in our ages."

He went on talking about her like I was one of his buddies. I guess the poor guy got lonesome sometimes and needed to talk.

"There are some funny things about Kitty, too."

"What do you mean, sir?"

"Did you ever notice the diamond she wears?"

"Yes, sir. It's about the biggest one I ever saw."

"She won't wear it to the hospital."

I thought back to the time she had come to see me in the hospital. She had not worn the ring then and I remembered that she had taken it off and put it in her pocketbook the time we took David to the hospital when he was in a coma.

"I guess she doesn't want to show it off in front of the nurses she went to school with. Might make them think she married you for your money."

"That's not the reason. I didn't give it to her."

"Oh?"

"No, she had that before we were married. I've never been able to find out where she got it. Her parents certainly couldn't have given it to her."

He didn't talk anymore.

There was a lot I didn't know about Kitty, too. I decided to ask her about the ring the next time I saw her.

I let him out at the hotel entrance and then got back in the car to wait for him. I turned the radio on and smoked a cigarette. I got to going over the whole plan, how I would go by the store on Broadway for some cigarettes, then pretend the car was out of order when I got on Catalpa. I would go back to the trunk, take out the shotgun, shoot David and give the gun to Kitty. It was a very simple and fool-proof plan. While I sat there smoking my cigarette I got to thinking about the gun in the trunk. I wasn't certain that I had loaded it. I tried to think back about my actions the night before, but I couldn't remember.

It would sure be one fine note if I pointed the gun at him and got only a dull click when I pulled the trigger.

After a while I couldn't stand it any longer. I got out of the car and went around to the back. I looked up and down the street. There was no one walking my direction so I opened the trunk and checked the gun. It was loaded all right. I had the safety on. I would have to remember to take it off safety before I pointed it at him. I closed the trunk. My hands were trembling and when I pulled the key out of the lock, it slipped out of my fingers and fell through a manhole opening.

I said a string of four letter words.

"What's the matter," the doorman asked. He had just come back to his place in front of the hotel entrance.

"I dropped my damned keys down the manhole."

We both got down on our knees and tried to see the keys.

"What's the matter?" David said as he came out and saw us down there on our knees.

"I dropped the keys."

"Then I'll call a taxi and go on home while you look for them." I could tell he was in a bad humor. I guess he thought somebody was pulling a practical joke on him with the phony call from the office. I'll bet he thought it was somebody in his own house, too.

"I'll have them in just a minute, sir." I said. I stood up and helped him in the car.

"Be quick about it," he said.

By that time a crowd was gathered around the manhole. Oh, Christ, I thought.

I hooked a couple of fingers down through the top and heaved the cover away. The key had a chain and goodluck piece attached to it that had caught on one of the wires that ran through the manhole. I lay down on the street, leaned down into the hole and got the key.

The policeman was telling the crowd to shove off. I pulled the top back in place, brushed some of the dirt off my clothes and got back in the car.

David was still mad.

"I thought you were supposed to be my body guard," he said as I put the key in the ignition and started the motor.

"I'm sorry, sir."

"Leave me sitting out there with a crowd like that gathered around."

I told him I was sorry again.

The whole thing had made me nervous. I was tied up enough before, but after that it was all the worse.

As I drove on up Michigan Avenue to the Outer Drive my nerves quieted down a little and I got the strange feeling that it was not me in the car. I was just a character in a movie who was going to shoot a guy. It didn't seem real.

I kept going over the plan in my mind. It had to be perfect. My life depended on its being perfect.

At last we got to the Foster Avenue cutoff. I kept on west on Foster instead of turning right into Sheridan Road.

"Where are you going?" David asked. He was still mad about being called downtown and then having to wait for me to find the keys.

"Mrs. Grey needs some cigarettes."

"You can get them later. Take me home first."

"Mrs. Grey asked me to be sure and get some for her."

"Well, get them later."

"I'm sorry, sir, but it's too late for me to turn."

"Damn it, what's up?" It was the first time I had ever heard him swear.

"Nothing, sir."

"Then take me home."

I didn't answer him. He knew something was screwy. He just sort of sensed it, I guess. Now I had to kill him because he would be suspicious if he lived and I wouldn't get another chance.

Like I said, I didn't pay any attention to him when he told me to take him straight home.

I turned right on Broadway and double parked in front of a cigar store a couple of blocks up the street. I took the keys with

me to make sure he wouldn't drive away. I felt so funny inside
that I can hardly remember even going into the store.

He was so mad he was red in the face when I got back in the car.

"Mike, you're fired," he said when we drove away. That was
all he said.

And I thought it was the last thing he would say. It was sort
of funny, him firing me. He didn't know that he was going to be
dead in three more minutes.

I watched close. When we got to Catalpa I turned east. I
pushed the accelerator pedal down hard a couple of times so it
seemed like there was something the matter with the engine. We
crossed Kenmore and I saw Kitty parked across the street ready
to take the gun and get away. I stopped the car.

"Something's wrong with the motor," I said and pulled the
car up to double park. "I'll have a look under the hood."

He didn't say anything.

I opened the car trunk. As I reached for the gun I could feel
my head getting bigger and smaller like somebody was blowing up balloons inside my skull and then letting out the air and
blowing them up again.

"What's the matter?" a deep voice said to me from a car that
had just eased up beside the Caddy.

It felt like I jumped five inches in the air. I looked up and
saw a police car with two policemen. I let go the gun and got the
wrench that was on the floor.

"Something's wrong with the engine," I said and could feel
the trembling come out in my voice.

"Need any help?"

"No thanks."

I watched them drive on down the street towards Sheridan
Road. Then I lifted the hood and poked around inside for a couple of minutes like I was fixing something.

I closed the hood and looked around. Kitty was still parked across the street. I wondered if David had spotted her yet. He was sitting up very stiff and looking straight ahead. There were no people on the street to see me. Now was the time to get the gun and blow David's head off. He wouldn't be mad much longer.

I opened the trunk again, put down the wrench and decided to have another look around just to be sure no one was watching.

I saw a jeep turn out of the Shell Oil Station on the comer and head our way. The cops had told somebody there that we needed help.

I closed the trunk.

"What's the matter?" the guy in the jeep asked when he got to us.

"I got it fixed."

"Go on and try it," he said.

I started the engine and drove off. David wouldn't get killed on that trip and it was going to be hard to get him in a spot like that again.

CHAPTER FIFTEEN

B Y THE TIME I got to my room I damn near had the shakes. I had been able to control myself and feel impersonal about it all up until then. But I was all keyed up for the kill and when it didn't come off things sort of piled up inside of me.

I threw myself down on the bed and gasped for air like I had run back from the Loop. There didn't seem to be enough air in the whole world. At last I covered my face with my arms and tried to feel dead again and fall asleep. But I was too restless to stay that way. I went to the bathroom and then walked back and forth beside the bed, striking my head with my closed fist like I could jar something out of my brain that was bothering me. It took three tries at striking a match before I got one to light a cigarette. There was only a couple of fingers of rot gut left in my fifth bottle. I finished that off, but it wasn't enough to even dent the edge of my feelings.

One thing I knew. I didn't want anything more to do with the job. Kitty could take her sex and go someplace else and she could take the ten million too. It wasn't worth going through what I felt. No dame or nothing was worth that.

I tried to think of some way to see Kitty, but things just wouldn't work right inside of my head. I couldn't plan what to do next. I thought of throwing my stuff together and pulling out, but I couldn't even plan things enough to do that. One thing I did know: I had to have a drink pretty quick or I would go nutty as a French fruit cake.

I put on my coat and stumbled down the steps and on out the drive to Sheridan Road. Somehow I got across the street in spite of all the traffic and then I walked on down towards Foster without even knowing where I was going. When I got to a grogshop near the corner of Sheridan and Foster I went in and bought a couple of pints of rot gut, shoved one in each of my coat pockets and walked down to the lake. I sat down on the rocky breakwater and opened the first bottle. I don't remember drinking it, but I remember I felt better by the time I heaved the empty bottle overboard. Before opening the second bottle I got up from the breakwater and pulled my dead body under a heavy green bush that grew about ten feet from the edge of the water. I took a couple of drinks from the second bottle and went to sleep.

After going to sleep under the bush down by the lake I stayed there a couple of hours. When I woke up it was dark and I could see the running lights on the yachts out on the lake.

I took another drink and got up. My clothes were all wrinkled and I had dirt in my hair and smeared over my face. At first I couldn't remember what had happened to me and then it all began to come back.

As I walked back towards Foster Avenue, I tried to think ahead and decide what I was going to do. I had come back to Chicago to get in something good so I could finally make a few bucks and quit throwing away my life, but now I was right back to where I had started. Maybe I'd always be a jerk who would always slide back to where I started. Some guys are like that. Nothing ever turns out right.

I was lonesome till I remembered Ruth and wondered what she was doing. She was the only good thing that had ever come into my life. Just being around her made me feel good inside. Suddenly I wanted to put my head in her arms and tell her all about everything. Somehow I was sure she would understand.

I dragged myself in the nearest drug store and gave Ruth a buzz. The house mother said she was not in, but that she expected her back by ten o'clock.

"Do you know where I can reach her?"

"I'm sorry, but I can't give you that information. May I give her a message for you when she comes in?"

"Thanks but I'll call back," I said and told her goodbye.

I looked at my watch. It was almost nine o'clock. What was I going to do the rest of the night?

I walked down Sheridan a couple of blocks to a hotel where I went to the men's room and cleaned up.

Then I got to thinking about Danny and his strip joint. Sure Danny had sent a couple of apes around to beat me up, but I didn't blame him. After all I had run off with one of his women and I had a beating coming for that. Besides Danny was probably drunk anyway when he told the boys to pay me a social call. The beating was my own fault. After all Danny was the only friend I had in Chicago outside of Ruth and I couldn't find her. Danny would be opening up his joint just about then and I decided to go by and chew the rag with him for a few minutes before calling Ruth again.

It was hot downtown. When I walked up the subway steps to Grand Avenue the hot damp air oozed up around me like a fog. By the time I reached Clark Street I was sweating so hard I had to take off my coat.

Danny's strip joint hadn't changed any. I sat down at the long horseshoe shaped bar and ordered a brew. It was early and the place was only half filled with degenerates. A girl up on the stage was starting her number, but neither she nor the band had their hearts in it.

"If you knew Susie
Like I know Susie…"

She was singing only she twisted the words around and made a dirty song out of it.

The beer was nice and cold. It was the only good thing I had hit all day. I ordered another one and asked the bar hop if Danny was in. He said he was out back so I took the bottle up and walked back to the office.

Danny was sitting there at his desk playing solitaire. He had his coat off so you could see his beer belly hanging out in front of him like a cow catcher. He had a cigar in the corner of his mouth.

"If it's not Sir Galahad," he said, looking up at me.

"That's right." I pulled up a chair and sat down.

"Didn't think I'd see you again."

"I guess I had it coming to me."

"Yeah, you sure did."

"Ruth's sister still around?"

"She left a couple of weeks ago. Full time hustler now." He relighted his cigar, threw the match on the floor and looked at me. "How're you and Ruth getting along?"

"Haven't seen much of her."

"Very noble."

"Maybe. You're going to leave her alone?"

"Yeah, I figure we came out about even on that deal," Danny said.

He went on laying down the cards on top of others.

"Still working for that guy up on Sheridan?"

"That's right."

"He must have a pile of dough. We ought to figure someway to get a little of it."

"I got fired today."

"Same old Mike."

"What do you mean?"

"Everything you touch turns to dirt. Why don't you put a bullet through your head and call it quits? Some guys like you always going around from one thing to the next. Nothing ever turns out right for them. Jerks. Here you are thirty years old. Got no car, got no house, got no business, got no money. I'll bet you haven't even got a woman."

That made me burn inside. I'd been saying the same thing to myself and it made me mad enough when I said it, but it made me a hundred times madder when he said it. The hell of it was that everything he said was true. I sure took the wrong turn every time I came to a fork in the road.

"Still want to go straight like you said when you came back from L.A.?" he asked.

"I want to make some money. You're right. I haven't got a lousy thing. Have you got a place for me somewhere in your setup?"

"Does it have to be strictly on the up and up?" He pushed his chair back from the table a little and looked at me over the end of the cigar butt that stuck in his mouth.

"No, it doesn't have to be strictly legitimate."

"So you've changed?"

"That's right. I've changed. I can't go on like this the rest of my life. I want something just like other guys."

He leaned back and laughed.

"Sorry, Mike, I got nothing for you in my setup."

"What do you mean?"

"Just what I said."

"Still sore about the dame I stole from you?" I asked.

"Naw, that don't mean nothing to me anymore. I got over that."

"Then what's the matter?"

"I already told you. You're a jerk and I don't want no jerks in business with me."

I downed the bottle of beer I held in my hand and got up.

"See you around, Mike," he said as I was leaving.

"Yeah," I said and went back through the strip joint where the babes were sweating it out.

I hit the bar next door and got a couple of drinks. Then I sort of worked my way north on Clark Street. I was too restless to stay long at any one place so I'd breeze in a joint, have a couple and work my way on up the street.

I kept trying to forget about myself, and then when I couldn't forget about the kind of person I was I tried to figure myself out, to put my finger on the reason for everything always going wrong for me.

I couldn't figure that out so I just kept hitting the joints. I wasn't feeling much pain by the time I got to North Avenue.

For a while I just stood there on the corner, half blind to the cars that swished past me.

"Jerk," I said to myself after a while and got in a taxi to go home.

I said the same word over and over to myself when I got to my place and looked at myself in the mirror. I took another drink, lit a fag and sat down on the edge of my bed with my elbows on my knees. I had been there long enough to pull the fag down about an inch when the door opened and Kitty came in. She had on a nightgown and slippers. Her blonde hair was falling down over her face and she looked upset. She brushed the hair out of her face and ran over to where I lay on the bed. I could feel her tremble as she put her arms around me and held me close to her.

"What's the matter, kid?" I asked her.

"Just hold me close to you, Mike."

I held her there for a minute or two and then looked at her face. She was crying and biting her lower lip. It was no act.

"What happened?"

"David."

"What did he do?"

"The same thing he always does."

"What?"

"He wants me to do those things again."

"The dirty bastard."

"Mike, you've got to kill him."

I knew I would kill him. I'd show Danny and everybody else that I could start one thing and follow it through to the end. When I got David's money I would buy up Danny's place and kick him out. I'd show all the sons of bitches that I wasn't a jelly fish after all. No. I was Mike Callahan, a guy who had what it took.

"Where is he now?" I asked Kitty.

"Upstairs in his room."

"Is anybody around?"

"No." She was looking up at me with her big blue eyes like I was God.

"Do you think we can get away with it if I kill him now?"

"We could say someone from the syndicate sneaked in the house and shot him."

"Yeah, we could," I said. I was too drunk and crazy and mad to see the holes in it. I didn't care about a master plan any longer. I didn't care about anything except killing David and showing everybody what kind of guts I had. So they called me a jerk. I'd show all of them.

"Let's go," I said. I checked my heater and took off the safety catch.

We walked quietly up the big front stairs and Kitty showed me which room he was in.

I found him asleep on his side of the big double bed. He was snoring and his open mouth looked little, surrounded by his fat face. His grey hair was all messed up but there was a little clearing where the pink skin showed through right in front of his ear.

I pulled the gun out and held it close. He must have heard me moving about because right then he opened his eyes and looked at me.

The sight of his eyes upset me so I must have blanked out for a minute. When I came to half of his brains made a bloody mess on the drapes across the room. The power of the forty five was so terrific it spun him around and shoved the top half of his body off the bed. I saw his arms and legs twitch a couple of times and then he was still.

Karl, dressed in a maroon smoking jacket, stepped from the closet.

"Mike, you're a very good shot," he said.

"Let me have the gun," Kitty said. Without wondering why she wanted it, I handed it over.

CHAPTER SIXTEEN

SUDDENLY I was very sober.

"Give me the gun," I said to Kitty.

"Stay where you are," she said and pointed the gun at me.

"What's going on here?" I asked.

"Don't you get the picture?" Karl said. He lighted a cigarette and began pacing back and forth in front of me.

"I smell a dirty frame."

"Do you now?" He turned to Kitty. "Bright boy, isn't he?"

"Very bright, but it's too late. Mike, we're going to turn you in for murdering David."

"You can't get away with it."

"Oh, yes I can. It was your gun. Both Karl and I saw you kill him. You had the motive because he fired you today."

Lights were flashing through my brain so fast I couldn't think. I knew that there was some way out. There was always a way out of everything if you could just figure it right. I tried to make the lights in my brain go away so I could start thinking again.

"You mean you're in love with Karl?" I asked, stalling for time.

"That's right. I've always been fond of, shall we say, mature men."

"Old men. Karl, she'll do the same thing to you some day. Don't you see the pattern?"

"Let me worry about that," he said. He didn't seem to be worried about anything. He had Kitty and he had the ten million green backs that went with her.

Kitty kept the gun leveled at me while Karl walked over to the phone that sat on the night table by the bed.

"Wait a minute," I said. I tried to think. Now there were no more lights flashing through my brain. In place of them I had pictures, crazy pictures of old men and young girls and guns and red blood. Pictures were better than lights. They were nearer to thinking.

"Well?" he said.

"Put the phone down. I have something to say that will interest you." Oh, Christ, let me think of something, I thought.

"All right, tell me what you have on your mind," he said, lifting the phone off the hook.

"He's just bluffing. Go ahead and call the police," Kitty said. She still stood there dressed in the nightgown with her legs spread apart and pointing the gun at me.

Karl began dialing the number. I started to walk over to him. I knew there was something I must tell him, but I couldn't remember what it was.

"Hold it," I said.

"Hello, I'd like ..." he said.

"It's about Kitty," I said.

He asked the desk sergeant to hold the line a minute.

"Make it quick," he said.

"Ask Kitty where she got her diamond ring," I said. I still don't know where the words came from, but suddenly I knew they were the right words to say.

"David gave it to me," she said.

"That's a lie. Ask her why she won't ever wear it when she goes to the hospital," I said.

Karl told the desk sergeant that he would call back later and hung up.

"If you turn me in I'll tell them that you were an accomplice," I said to Kitty. "I'll tell them to investigate the ring, too. How would you like that?"

Karl stood looking at Kitty like he expected her to explain it all.

"We'll have to kill him," she said.

"Maybe that would be best," Karl said. I began edging over toward Kitty so I could make a dive for the gun.

"Go in the other room," she said. Karl turned stiffly and went out through the door.

For a second her eyes followed him. I dived for the gun. An explosion blinded me and almost blew out my ear drums, but I had my hands on the gun. When it went off the second time it was pointed straight up at the ceiling and the flash blinded both of us. I wrenched the gun from her hand and staggered over to the door. My eyes were burning and I could hardly see the outline of the room.

Karl was standing in the hall.

"If you try to pin this on me. I'll kill both of you," I said. I went over to the staircase and began feeling my way downstairs. By the time I reached the street the sight in my right eye was coming back.

I put the gun in my pocket and ran across Sheridan Road like a scared animal. I ran over to Kenmore and turned south. By the time I reached Foster I had come to my senses enough to remember that a running man was more suspicious than one who was walking. My legs ached like a sore tooth but I still wanted to run so bad that it was all I could do to force myself to walk. As I crossed Sheridan again and made my way toward the lake I began to wake up more. My left shoulder had taken the first shot. It would not move and I could feel the blood running down my arm and soaking in the coat sleeve. My face was on fire from the powder bum caused by the second shot.

Finally I made the lake where I heaved the gun as far out over the water as I could. Then I crawled under the bush where I had passed out earlier that day.

It wasn't the coziest night I ever spent. While stopping the blood with a handkerchief stuffed in the torn flesh of my shoulder, the sirens started screaming down the Outer Drive. I wondered what Kitty was telling them. It was my bet that she would try to shove it off on the syndicate boys. At least that was what she would do if she was smart.

By the time things had quieted down some and I was beginning to relax a little, it started to rain. At first the fine mist didn't get to me, but after about a half hour went by the leaves were soaked and dripping on me. I huddled myself together the best I could, but by morning I was cold and wet and hungry. I knew what the word outcast meant. I didn't belong to anyone and I had no place to go. On top of that something from down inside me said: "You killed a man," every few minutes and it would send a sick feeling over me. For all I knew every cop in town was looking for me. I could see why guys would give themselves up just so they could be in a warm jail or be around people to talk with. It was the worst hell I had ever known, even worse than the cold clear nights I had spent in the Sahara Desert during my army days when I knew I was going up front to be shot at the next morning.

I didn't have a mirror or a tooth brush or soap or anything. By morning my mouth felt like fuzzy worms had been crawling in it all night. When it got light I took off my clothes and jumped in the cold lake water to wash the black powder marks off my face. My left eye was swollen shut and my arm was pounding like it was full of a million little devils driving stakes in the bone.

I had to get a place to stay. I couldn't go on sleeping under bushes and not eating. It was a chance I just had to take.

I sat down at the counter of a crummy cafe over on Broadway at about seven thirty. The Tribune ran headlines about the murder of David Grey. It told about him kicking the wire service system out of his hotel and how he had been so frightened of the syndicate that he had hired a bodyguard. The police suspected the syndicate was mixed up with the killing and they were busy rounding up several men who were known hoodlums. On the back page there were pictures of the house, of Kitty and Karl. There was also a sketch of the room where the body had been found. After looking at all that I couldn't eat any breakfast. Instead I went to a tavern on the corner and downed a couple of quick ones that I chased with beer.

I got on the El that was crowded with office workers and rode down to the Near North Side because I was sure they would be looking for suspicious characters up north where David had been bumped off.

I wanted a cheap hotel room, but decided that was too public. I hit a string of crummy wooden boarding houses over on Hubbard Street not far from Dearborn. The first place I tried wasn't so hot. The man sitting back against the door in a wooden chair looked at me like he wanted to know what had happened. I turned and left without saying anything. There was another lousy joint in the next block that I decided to give a tumble. It was better. The fat sloppy woman who collected my rent money was so batty she wouldn't even be able to read the papers.

I laughed to myself when I saw the room. It was even worse than the flea trap I was living in up on Kenmore when I first met

Kitty. Yeah, I'd come a long way. I fell over the iron bed and it sounded like a mortar shell landing in a mess of barbed wire.

I lay still for a long time looking up at the streaked ceiling, hoping that the pain in my shoulder would make me pass out for a few hours. After about an hour I got to the half awake-half asleep stage and suddenly there was the scream of a siren outside on the street. I jumped to my feet and ran to the window. It was a cop all right, but he was just stopping a car for speeding.

When you've killed somebody a siren makes you go weak all over and you want to throw up. Your ticker starts in like a riveting machine and you live for a while in hell.

This time I couldn't get back to sleep. I kept turning from side to side looking for a comfortable spot, but there weren't any. Then I got to thinking about all the things that could happen to a wound like mine. I wondered if the bullet was still in my arm and if I'd get lead poisoning from it like the joke said. Then I wondered about tetanus and gangrene. That day I saw myself in some awful pictures, but the worst ones were about my eye. My left eye was swollen tight shut so I couldn't even see light. I wondered if I would lose it and if the other one would gradually dim out on me like it did sometimes in the stories I heard. I could see myself sitting on the corner of State and Randolph. My left arm would be gone and I would be blind as I held out a dirty hat full of pencils for people to buy.

No, you can't go to sleep when your skull's full of things like that. Finally I drove those thoughts away, but the ones that took their place were even worse. I saw David again as he looked at me just before I blew his brains out. I saw Kitty and Karl having a drink together and laughing at me.

"Christ, leave me alone," I said out loud and got up from the bed.

As I walked the floor my stomach was gurgling from hunger, but still the very thought of food nauseated me. I couldn't go no like that much longer. I had to have a drink.

I didn't meet anybody on the street outside and the grog shop on the corner was deserted. For once I'd been lucky.

When I got back to my room I was trembling and out of breath from climbing the two flights of stairs. Yes, I would get a nice drunk on if I finished that fifth bottle in my weakened condition. But I didn't care about how drunk I got. I just wanted to get away from the pain and the pictures. I didn't give a damn if I never woke up.

I ripped off the plastic seal around the neck of the bottle and sat down on the edge of the bed as I unscrewed the top and put the smooth glass top against my mouth.

Yes, that was what I needed. I lay back down on the bed and put the open bottle there on the floor beside me so I could reach it for another long drink. I kept that up till I passed out.

CHAPTER SEVENTEEN

W HILE I slept a word kept coming back to me.

That word was Ruth. It ran around inside my head like the ball on a roulette wheel. And the word had a feeling that went with it. It felt warm and soft and secure. It wasn't a feeling like being in love. Maybe it was more like the feeling a little kid has for its mother. It was the only thing that could make me feel good right then.

When I woke up it was dark and I lay there on the bed for a few minutes letting the word run around somemore because it felt good. I put my arm around the pillow on the bed and hugged it to me as I said the one word: "Ruth."

I thought of her with her soft auburn hair and shy soft smile. I wondered what would have happened to me if I had married her and settled down to punching a timeclock some place. If I had done that, I would have turned out to be just another jerk lost in the millions of jerks who punch timeclocks twice a day. But I would have had something real. Now I was a very special person set apart from the common run of men. I was famous. I was a murderer.

I went to the dirty bathroom at the end of the hall and threw some cold water over my face. I just felt half human when I went back to the grog shop on the corner to give Ruth a ring.

"I can't hear you," she said when I started speaking.

"It's Mike."

"Oh, hello, Mike."

"Ruth, will you do me a favor?"

"Just name it."

"Will you come down to my place? I want to talk to you."

"Is it important that I come tonight?"

"Yes."

"Then give me the address."

I told her the address on Hubbard Street slow so she could write it down.

"Aren't you still working on Sheridan Road?"

"No. Haven't you read the papers?"

"No."

"There's been some trouble. Don't tell anybody that you're coming to meet me."

"Whatever you say," she said in a puzzled voice.

"And Ruth."

"Yes?"

"Pick up an evening paper and some sandwiches for me on your way."

We told each other good-bye and I went back to my room where I lay back down on the rickety bed. Just talking to her made me feel better.

I went to sleep and then later jumped up ready to fight when I heard a noise at my door. It was Ruth dressed in a candy striped dress that should have made her look thin like the kid I had first met. But she had filled out and you could tell she was getting to be more of a woman every day.

I dragged back to the bed and sagged down on it.

"Mike, what's happened to you?" she said when the naked overhead light showed my face.

"Oh, hell," I said. That wasn't what I wanted to say at all but that was all that would come out. I put my head up against her and cried like a baby.

I tried to stop. I bit my lip and clinched my fists but it wasn't any use. I shook all over and the tears came out like they had been damned up there inside me all my life. I must have cried ten minutes like that.

"Do you want to tell me about it?" she asked.

I managed to stop crying enough to talk.

"I got framed. I told you about Kitty, the girl who was married to my boss."

"Yes."

"I fell in love with her and she framed me."

"What happened?"

"She talked me into killing her husband and after it was all over I found out that she and the valet were using me to get the old man out of the way. It was so simple and stupid. How a guy that's been around as much as I have could fall for a trick like that, I'll never know. You'd think I'd get some sense in my head, but instead I get dummer everyday.

"I always want to be the big shot. I came back from L.A. dead broke and made up my mind to get somewhere. I saw a chance at ten million dollars and I jumped for it. I've always been a wash-out at everything."

"Mike, you weren't a failure."

"I never made any money."

"Most people never do make any money, but that doesn't mean they're failures. They just go along paying the rent and doing the best they can. They aren't failures. They're the heroes."

"I got all mixed up somewhere along the line."

I opened up the paper she held in her hand and read where the cops were looking for an ex-bodyguard named Mike Callahan for questioning. There was still no mention of my name in connection with the killing. The police were holding several suspects for a lie detector test.

"What are you going to do now?" she asked.

"I don't know. I'm so weak that I can't even think straight."

"Did you eat anything today?"

"No."

"Would you like me to go out and get you some soup?" She looked over at the sandwiches she had brought. "You should have something hot. The sandwiches will keep till tomorrow."

"I'm hungry but I'm not sure I can keep anything down."

"Will you try?"

"Sure," I said. She lighted a cigarette for me and then went out to shop. It was good to see Ruth again. She took over like a mother robin with a nest full of young ones and it was good to have somebody around who cared, somebody I could be sure about.

The soup tasted good and I was able to keep it down. She brought back a package of medical supplies and started to work on my arm about an hour after I had eaten. It was the first good look I had had at the bullet hole. The flesh at the tip of the shoulder was torn away so that the ragged edges of the muscles was all that was left. She poured some hot stuff over it and then bandaged it. Just smelling the disinfectant and seeing the white bandages made it feel better. She put some ointment over my eye.

"Can you go to sleep now?" she asked when I gave a sigh and lay back down on the bed.

"I think so."

"Do you want me to stay with you?"

"Won't they kick you out of the girl's club if you stay out all night?"

"Yes."

"And you don't care?"

"Yes, I care, but I care more about you."

"Ruth, why was I such a fool?"

She didn't say anything. She just looked at me with her big eyes and I knew all the more that I had been such a fool. I had loved Ruth all the time. I must have loved her. She was the only person in the world I ever went out on the limb to help. But I had been such a fool. I had thrown everything away when I could have had Ruth and a nice little home someplace.

"Darling," I said, "Give me your hand."

She stretched out her long moist hand and I took it in mine.

"Ruth."

"Yes."

"I love you," I said and squeezed her hand.

"And I love you too."

"When did you start loving me?" I asked.

"That first night when we left the apartment and sat over by the lake to watch the sun come up. I felt so little and helpless, but I had you beside me. I knew you would help me. I trusted you. I could just feel the goodness inside you."

"The only time in the world I ever had any goodness was when I was with you. You always brought out what little goodness I had."

"You're full of goodness," she said like she really believed it. It was nice to have someone like Ruth believe I was an all right guy. "When did you fall in love with me?"

"I guess it was that first night."

"What about Kitty?"

"It wasn't love with Kitty. It was something else. It was almost like we hated each other and rubbed our bodies together to kill the hate. It was excitement, but it wasn't love."

I lighted another cigarette and took a long drag.

"But I wasn't sure that I loved you until I got this wound. After that you were the one I wanted. You are everything I have in the whole world."

I had another drink, Ruth brought a towel in for me to wash with and then we cut out the light and went to bed.

I thought we would go to sleep, but when I felt her sweet warmth against me I wanted to be closer and closer to her. Once I had felt tenderness and goodness with Kitty, but it had been all a fake: a fake feeling with a fake person. Now I knew what I felt was real. Ruth was good. She even made me feel good.

"I want to be near you," I whispered.

"And I want you near."

I kissed her lips and her neck and breathed in the perfume from her body as she pushed up against me, trembling.

"Are you afraid?" I asked.

"A little. Wouldn't any girl be afraid at a time like this?"

"I guess so." I explored her with my fingers. "Do you want me to stop?"

"No."

"You're sure?"

In the dark I could feel her nod her head.

"I'll be slow and careful."

"I know you will."

Now I could feel her really trembling. I was careful, but still she couldn't help giving a little cry of pain.

"Darling, I'm sorry." My voice was trembling too.

"Don't be sorry."

Her body was locking around mine. Now I had freed her from something and the fear was draining away and minute by minute she was becoming a woman and she was more woman and more woman and more woman and then we were falling down the stairs together as our bodies melted together and then suddenly for each of us it was all and all and all and we were lying beside each other breathing hard as we came back to this world again.

"Mike, I adore you."

"I love you Ruth."

And then after awhile:

"Don't be frightened. I'll take care of you."

"I know you will."

"And I'll try to be a better person. You help me and I'll try hard."

"I will."

She turned over and put her head on my shoulder and we went to sleep that way.

CHAPTER EIGHTEEN

RUTH spent the night with me. It was a night like I had never known before. The next morning I felt like I'd been touched by an angel.

But the shoulder was bad. Now it was swollen so that I could feel every one of my heart beats pound against it.

"Do you still love me?" Ruth asked. It's funny how women all think you won't love them anymore if you sleep with them.

"More than ever. What about you?"

"I worship you like you were a God."

"Forget it. I'm not."

"You were very tender and sweet."

I laughed. Who would ever think about me being tender and sweet? Danny would really get a buzz out of it if he could hear her say that about me.

"I'm just another jerk and you're crazy to be in love with me."

"I know I'm crazy."

"But you still love me?"

"Yes."

"Then it must be love."

I moved over to kiss her and she saw my face twist with the pain I felt from the shoulder.

"Is it your shoulder?"

"Yes, it hurts worse this morning."

She got out of bed and took the bandage off. I didn't have to look at it to know that it was bad. I could smell it. She put her hand against my forehead and said that I had a fever.

"You've got to see a doctor."

"Fat chance. No doctor would take care of a bullet wound like that without reporting it. Just pour some more of that red stuff on and bandage it."

She looked at it closer.

"Darling, that won't help. The infection's way deep inside. Nothing I put on the outside will help that."

"Maybe you could get some penicillin from the druggist. Ask him how much to give and everything."

"He won't let me have it without a prescription."

"Tell him your grandmother's sick and you can't get a doctor to come to the house."

"I'll try," she said and slipped a dress over her head to go to the bathroom down the hall. She brought me a glass of water and a wet towel to wash with. After that she finished dressing and went out to the drug store.

I got out of bed and went over to the dresser where I kept the whiskey. Yeah, I was sweet and tender as hell, I thought as I turned the bottle up and drank about three inches. Yeah, I was sweet all right.

The druggist wouldn't let her have any penicillin. He told her to have the doctor telephone him.

"Here's the morning paper," she said and put it down on the bed beside me. She looked tired.

GREY'S BODYGUARD SOUGHT IN KILLING

the big black headlines said. Now I was famous at last.

My hands shook so I had to put the paper flat on the bed to read it. I almost wish I hadn't read it.

I was named in David Grey's will to the amount of a hundred thousand dollars! Kitty had changed her story around and told them she thought I had heard of the will and killed him for the money. They were just a couple of sweet innocent people who had been taken in by a sharpie.

Now I was rich—

and I'd never be able to touch the money, not with a hundred foot pole. Yes, I was getting my reward all right: the kind of reward you get for the kind of life I'd led.

"Mike, what are you going to do?" Ruth asked after I had finished the paper.

"I don't know. I'm so damn sick and weak I can't even think straight. What do you want me to do?"

"That's up to you," she said.

"Would you go with me if I made a run for it?"

"Yes."

"You're nuts."

"Mike I do love you. But I love you too much to see you lie there and get blood poisoning."

I had to have some treatment for my shoulder and I had to have it soon.

Danny would know all about the kind of doctors who would fix me up without asking any questions. I didn't want him to find out I was with Ruth, but there didn't seem to be any other way.

"You'd better call Danny and tell him I need a doctor," I said.

"I'm afraid of him. Maybe he'll tell Fran where I am and I'll have to go back with her."

"Don't worry, baby, I'll take care of you. Run call Danny and tell him to send a doctor around to fix up this shoulder."

While Ruth was out making the call I began to get the shakes. Every muscle in my body began quivering like I was standing naked on a windy street corner with the temperature twenty below. I tried to light a fag, but my hand shook so the match waved out before I could take a draw. I gave up on the smoking and threw my twisted body across the bed to wait for Ruth. I guess I must have gone to sleep or something because when she came back it took me a couple of minutes to recognize her and remember what was going on with us.

"Danny said he would call somebody," Ruth said.

"He'd do what?"

"He'll get a doctor for you."

"Yeah, I remember now. Did he recognize your voice?"

"Yes," she said and looked away from me like she didn't want to talk about it any more.

"What did he say to you?"

"Nothing."

I could tell by the look on her face that she didn't want to talk about it, but I wanted to know what he had said so I could guess how he would treat her the next time they met.

"Out with it. What did he say?"

"He said that he had something for me."

"The dirty rotten dog. Don't get near him unless I'm with you."

But a lot of good I would be in a fight right then.

Ruth wet a towel with some cold water and began wiping my feverish face now that the chilling had stopped. I wished that the whole world would go away and leave us alone together like we were then. If I ever got out of the mess I was in, things would certainly be different with me. It made me sick to think how different things would be right then if I had dropped Kitty and gone off with Ruth the first time I met her. She brought out all the good in me and Kitty brought out all the bad.

"It's a damned shame," I said, half delirious with fever.

"What is?"

"That I didn't fall in love with you sooner."

"It's still not too late," she said and I hoped she was right. "You should have known better than to get mixed up with someone like Mrs. Grey, but now that part is all over and things will be better."

She said it like I had only been a bad boy and gotten in a fight at school. But how could she stand me? Didn't she realize I had killed a man?

Suddenly the sound of sirens came up from the street below. Ruth rushed to the window.

"They're just giving it to some jerk for speeding," I said.

"Mike, there're two police cars stopping out in front of the building."

My friend Danny must have turned me in. Maybe there was a two cent reward out for me and Danny sure wouldn't miss a chance to make two cents. I knew that something had to be done. I made myself sit up on the edge of the bed, but that was as far ahead as I could think. My mind was too burned up from the fever to go on from there. And then I felt Ruth's hands pulling me to my feet and quickly helping me through the door that led into the hall. I followed her to the bathroom at the end of the hall and we were half-way out the bathroom window and on the roof of the next building before I fully realized what was going on. She helped me across the roof to the next building where we went down the fire escape to the street below.

"You can make it," Ruth kept saying to me as we walked. "You can make it."

"Make it to where? I might just as well throw in the towel, Ruth. It's not good. I can't make it."

As I was saying these words I found myself stumbling down the steps leading to a subway station. Didn't she know that I wasn't worth this kind of trouble? She put me in the corner of the car and squeezed up tight against me to keep me from falling out of the seat into the aisle when the car started. I don't know how long we rode like that but it seemed like forever.

"Christ, it's not worth it," I said at last.

"We got off at the next stop," she said.

"Where are we going?"

"I'm going by the girls' club to borrow some money first and then we're going to Billings Hospital to get your shoulder taken care of."

"They'll turn me in to the cops when they hear it's a bullet wound."

"We won't tell them it was done by a bullet. The shoulder is swollen so much and so infected now that they won't be able to tell that it was caused by a bullet."

Maybe she was right, I thought, but I was too sick and tired to care what happened to me any longer. Finally I got up and let her shove me off of the El train onto the platform. She pushed me into a taxi downstairs and told him to go to the girls' club. I folded up in the back seat while she was inside trying to raise some dough. The driver must have wondered what was going on between us. I must have passed out or something because the next thing I remember I was sitting up in the cab seat and Ruth was slapping my face.

"We're at the hospital," she kept saying.

"All right, so we're at the hospital. Let me alone. I just want to die."

She and the driver helped me up to the door and Ruth held me there alone as she paid the cabbie and then rang the bell to call the nurse on emergency duty.

"Now remember not to say anything. I'll do all the talking. Do you hear me?"

"Yes," I said. Ruth was surprisingly adult and commanding about this whole thing. Maybe she was getting over this little girl stuff now that she had been in the city alone for awhile.

"Don't say a word."

"O. K., but don't keep telling me everything twice. I'm not a kid."

"I love you, Mike."

"You're nuts."

The door in front of me gave way so that Ruth had to catch me to keep me from falling on the floor.

I was so sick then that I hardly remember what went on. I remember that they got a sleepy looking intern who acted bored as hell as he filled out the accident report.

"How did you say it happened?" he asked Ruth and then ran a hand through his thick hair as though he were trying to hold his head up. The uniform he wore was still white but you could tell from the wrinkles that it had been slept in.

"We were hanging curtains last night when my husband slipped. The rod stuck in his shoulder."

The intern mumbled something.

"What did you say?" Ruth asked.

"Nasty way to get hurt."

The nurse helped me over to the table and took off my shirt while the intern finished filling out the report. It hurt like hell when he put a drain down in the tissue to keep the pus from backing up. After that he bandaged it up and told me to come back the next day.

"Should I give him a tetanus shot?" the nurse asked the intern.

"Never heard of anybody getting tetanus from a curtain rod," he said and yawned. "Just give him three hundred thousand units of penicillin and let him go home to bed."

"All right," the nurse said and suppressed a smile like there was some kind of joke between them about his bed.

After the nurse stuck me in the butt with the penicillin Ruth told them that we were on our way home in Iowa and wouldn't be able to come back for more penicillin and a fresh dressing the next day.

The intern was putting some papers away and didn't answer.

"What should these folks do, Dr. Farrer?" the nurse asked and then had to tell him that we wouldn't be able to get in the next day.

"Then give them some sulfa tablets."

The last thing I remember it was night again and I was on another train propped in the corner where I wouldn't fall off the seat. My shoulder was full of atom-hot fire and felt like it would explode any second.

CHAPTER NINETEEN

A
LL NIGHT I was awake enough to know that I was traveling; I felt Ruth pushing me about, making me walk or sit or climb stairs; but I was too sick to know just what was happening to me. Certainly I was too sick to care.

When I woke up it was like I had suddenly died and landed in another world. There were smooth clean sheets beneath me and the clean, bright sun was streaming in through an open window. Now the pain in my shoulder was gone.

"Ready for some more pills?" a voice asked me when I tried to sit up. It was a soft sweet voice and I knew that it was friendly towards me but I couldn't place it. When I tried to make my mind go back over what had happened to me, it cut off like an electric motor with a short in it. Maybe I felt too good right then to remember any of the bad part that had gone before.

"Here you go, two more pills and a glass of water."

"Ruth?"

"Who else would it be?"

"Yes, it's you, isn't it, Ruth. Thanks."

"For what?"

"Thanks for bringing me here and taking care of me."

"I'll bet you don't even know where we are. We've been here three days and this is the first time you've shown any interest."

"I might not know where it is, but I like it. Am I in the hospital?"

"Goodness no, that was ages ago when we were at the hospital."

"Well, I might not know where it is, but it's the nicest place I ever spent a night," I said, lay back down on the pillow and passed out again.

I dreamed of all kinds of evil things. There were sinister men chasing after me. One of the men who was fat and who had small slanting eyes was luring me to a cave that I knew would be full of unspeakable lewdness. I refused to go with him and then he had a beautiful blonde dancing girl come out to the mouth of the cave and dance for me, shedding her veils one by one and beckoning to me with her finger. As I touched her she turned into a haggard witch and the fat man laughed. He grabbed out for me like he was going to carry me down in the cave and then I struck back at him. We wrestled there at the mouth of the cave and at last I threw him to the ground and ran a sword through his chest.

"Mike, wake up," Ruth's voice was saying to me and she was slapping me on the face.

The other time when I woke up the room and I had been full of goodness and cleanness and it had seemed that there was nothing but goodness inside me, but this time when I woke up it was night time in the room as well as inside me. I suddenly remembered all that had gone before: Kitty and David, and the way I had killed him. Now I was filled with vileness.

"Are you awake?" Ruth asked and stopped slapping me.

"Yes."

"What was the matter?"

"I was dreaming about hell and then I woke up and remember everything that happened. I killed a man."

"That's all in the past."

"Is it?"

"Yes, you did many things in the past, but now that's all gone and we're going to find a new life together. We're going to have each other forever and that will make things right inside you."

"You should have turned me over to the cops or let me die on the streets."

"I love you, Mike."

"Why?"

"Maybe part of it is because you helped me one time when I needed you. The other part I can't explain."

"It's no good, Ruth. You'll ruin your life for nothing. If you'd stayed at work and left me alone, you might have had a chance, but this way you're getting the booby prize. I never should have called you, but I didn't know what to do. Now that I'm better why don't you leave me and try to forget you ever met me."

Then she sat down by the bed and began talking. She told me how much she loved me and said that we would work things out. The shooting of David had taken place because Kitty talked me into it. I had gotten mixed up with the wrong women and that was what really happened to me. It wasn't my fault, she said. All that was in the past. We were going somewhere downstate in Indiana and get a job on a farm where I wouldn't be around people like those I had known in Chicago. Maybe someday we would own our own place.

It was all a crazy dream, but I liked it. Ruth was so sold on the whole idea that she got me to believing it just might be possible.

The rest of the week I stayed there in the neat little room that was the tourist cabin she had rented near the Indiana Dunes. My strength came back fast and every day when she dressed the shoulder it looked better. Now I could see the arm without any pain at all. I finished taking the sulfa pills and then the fever didn't come back again so I knew I must be just about well. We'd been there six days when Ruth brought a Chicago Tribune back with her when she brought home the groceries. The story of David's death had dwindled to one column on page three. There was a summary of what had gone before. They were still looking for the chauffeur and there was a pretty good description of me but without a picture it wouldn't get them too far. I learned that Kitty and Karl were both free as the air without a trace of suspicion around them. That burned me up to think Kitty had been in love with Karl all the time and had just used me to get rid of her husband. Here they who had really done the killing were scot free to go about their lives while I had to keep away from the open and might have to spend all my life hiding. That time she had cut down on David's insulin had only been a fake to make me think she had tried to kill him.

I had gotten a lousy deal and I was going to do something about it.

The next day I got an idea. There had always been something screwy about Kitty and that big damn diamond that she wore. David had said that he didn't give it to her and that he was certain that her family could never have bought it. There must be something big in her past life that accounted for that stone. If I could get the cops to snooping around trying to pick up a lead on that it might take the heat off me and give Kitty and Karl a little of the kind of reward they had coming.

"Ruth, how far are we from Chicago?"

"About sixty miles."

"Will you do me a favor?" I asked.

"What do you think?"

"I want you to take a trip into Chicago and telephone the police station. Ask to speak to homicide and tell them to investigate the big diamond ring that Kitty Grey wears. Tell them it might have something to do with the time she was in nurse's training at Memorial Hospital."

Ruth said she would give them my message but she couldn't see what sense it made. I wasn't sure myself that it made sense but it seemed to be a strike in the right direction. It might do something to drive a wedge between Karl and Kitty. Any favors I could do for those characters would be strictly what they had coming to them. They expected to walk away from murder with clean hands and let me take the rap for everything. I had a jail record from the time I was in stir out on the coast and the jury would never take my word for anything. I could shout to the rafters that Karl and Kitty were accessories and nobody would ever believe me.

The day Ruth went to Chi I began to get restless. I was ready to move on now that my strength was returning. During the week or so that I had been out of circulation I had sprouted quite a respectable beard. I decided to keep the mustache. I gave myself a very short crew haircut and by the time I got through my old lady herself wouldn't have recognized me.

"Mike! What have you done to yourself?" Ruth said when she got back.

"I thought a little plastic job would be a good idea since I'm about ready to push on. This is too near the city to suit me. What do you say we head downstate tomorrow and start looking for a job?"

"All right."

"How did it go in the city?"

"The police tried to make me keep talking so they could trace the call I was making, but I hung up after I gave them the information about Mrs. Grey's diamond ring.

"Good kid."

It would be interesting to see what the newspapers had to say in the morning.

CHAPTER TWENTY

I F RUTH'S CALL to the police station had any effect on the case it wasn't mentioned in the Tribune the next morning. Now there was only a tiny paragraph on the fifth page.

But still I was a wanted man and every flat-foot in a dozen states would be on the lookout for me. I felt restless staying so close to Chicago and wanted to move on downstate Indiana where we could find a job on a farm that was away from things like cops.

That morning Ruth paid the rest of our bill there at the tourist court and we hopped the next bus south. With my cropped hair and mustache I hoped nobody would recognize me. Just to make things even more certain I bought a big straw beach hat at a novelty shop in front of the tourist court and after we got on the bus I pulled the hat over my face and lay back in the seat like I was sleeping. It wasn't a perfect way to make a run for it, but it was good enough because we got all the way to Plainsville, Indiana without any trouble. We planned to buy a local paper the next morning and look for a job on one of the farms not too far from the little town where we got a room at a very second class hotel.

When Ruth came in with the paper on the next morning it wasn't the want-ads of the local sheet that took our attention.

BUTLER KILLED DAVID GREY, the headlines of the Chicago Tribune read. That was a real switch. My hands shook as I read down the column. The cops started tracing down the diamond ring that Kitty wore and she got frightened. They discovered that Kitty had been dismissed from Memorial Hospital when she was a student nurse because a patient had died under mysterious circumstances. Also the patient had owned a large diamond ring that had never been located after her death. That would certainly explain how Kitty got the ring and why she would never wear it around the hospital. She must have been pretty nervous about her own life when the police were able to connect her with a possible murder in her past life. Now there was another dead person connected with her. Yes, she must have been nervous as hell. The newspaper went on to say that Mrs. David Grey confessed that she was in love with Karl the butler, and that he killed her husband so he could have her and the fortune that went with her.

"What do you make out of that?" Ruth asked from behind my back where she was reading over my shoulder.

"Don't you see what happened?"

"Not at all."

"They were going to accuse Kitty of murdering her husband, but she pulled a fast one and said that Karl did the killing."

"But why Karl? Why didn't she stick to her story about you doing it?"

"Because they weren't able to find me and Kitty knew the cops would come nearer leaving her alone if they had the murderer in their hands. She knew the cops would keep poking around looking for evidence as long as they didn't have the murderer."

It was hard to believe that I was now free to go out in the world again and walk the streets without worrying. I didn't feel too bad about Karl taking the rap for me. After all he had been in on the deal from the first and it may have been Karl who suggested the whole plan to Kitty. Certainly Karl had the most to gain by David's death.

I didn't like to look at myself as the guy who had committed the perfect murder. I didn't like to think of myself as a murderer and after a few days I had myself believing that it wasn't really me who did the killing. I had only been the instrument that the real murderer used.

The next day there was more news in the paper:

BLONDE WIFE HELD AS MURDERER

Putting the finger on Karl hadn't been very smart. He asked for a lie test and got one. Oh, he knew about what was going on all right and he would be an accessory, but he hadn't pulled the trigger and he wasn't going to the chair for it.

The newspaper went on to say how cool Kitty had been when she started her lie test. She must have been sure she could beat it, but she didn't. In the end she told the truth.

She had taken the gun from my hand, shot David and handed the gun back to me before Karl came in the room.

It must have all happened in that second that David opened his eyes and looked at me. I remember blanking out for a second and when I came to I held the gun and David's brains were over on the drapes. I hadn't done the killing after all.

I read on down the page and learned that the police had dug up some more facts about Kitty. They found out she had been working for Danny as a stripper before she went into nurses training. In a signed statement Danny said that she had always had a predilection for older men. Kitty hadn't been a very nice girl. The coppers had put two and two together and decided she was in on the deal to kill her husband. Any fool could see that it figured. She was a girl born to be bad and she was full of rottenness all the way through to the core.

The next column in the paper said that Danny's place had been closed down because it was contributing to the delinquency of minors by recruiting girls under eighteen as strippers.

All my friends were getting paid off with the kind of reward they deserved.

Ruth and I did a dance. That afternoon we got on the bus and headed back to Chicago.

When they strapped me up to the lie detector I knew if would be best for me to tell the truth.

"Now would you give us in your own words the exact story of what happened leading to the murder," the gentleman said.

"When I saw her come out of the building and head for my car I thought she was just another dizzy blonde," I began. "But I changed my mind when she got in with me. She wasn't just another blonde. There was something mean about her—like she was a real bawdy ...."

END

www.ingramcontent.com/pod-product-compliance
Lightning Source LLC
Chambersburg PA
CBHW050855180626
46814CB00007B/2755